Who's Jim Hines?

GREAT LAKES BOOKS

*A complete listing of the books in this series
can be found online at wsupress.wayne.edu*

Who's Jim Hines?

Jean Alicia Elster

Wayne State University Press / Detroit

12 11 10 09   5 4 3 2

Library of Congress Cataloging-in-Publication Data

Elster, Jean Alicia.
Who's Jim Hines? / Jean Alicia Elster.
p. cm. — (Great Lakes books)
Summary: In 1935 Detroit, a twelve-year-old African American boy
learns about the realities of racial injustice while working for his
father's wood company during the Great Depression.
ISBN 978-0-8143-3402-7 (pbk. : alk. paper)
1. African Americans—Juvenile fiction. [1. African Americans—Fiction.
2. Race relations—Fiction. 3. Depressions—1929—Michigan—Fiction.
4. Fathers and sons—Fiction. 5. Michigan—History—20th century—
Fiction.] I. Title. II. Title: Who is Jim Hines?
PZ7.E529Wh 2008
[Fic]—dc22

All photos courtesy of the Ford Family Archives

Sketch of donkey saw by Jean Ford Fuqua based on notes by
Douglas Ford Jr.

Designed and typeset by Maya Rhodes
Composed in Century Old Style Std and Clarendon MT

Contents

Acknowledgments

I want to extend my heartfelt gratitude to my uncle, Douglas Ford Jr., MD, my mother, Jean Ford Fuqua, and my aunt, Maber Ford Hill, for their willingness—once again—to share their story with me.

Sincere appreciation to my cousin, Cheryl Hanna, for originally "seeing" the story in a bit of family lore. Thanks to my son, Isaac Elster, my sister, Gwynn Fuqua, and my editor, Kathryn Wildfong, all of whose astute editorial comments helped bring this manuscript to its final form.

Also, thanks to the Ragdale Foundation for offering me a writer's residency where I could actually begin this book.

As always, my deepest gratitude is reserved for my husband, Bill, for his unfailing support and encouragement and for giving me the space to write.

Prologue

The Detroit I write about and the Detroit I live
in are two different places. Back in the 1930s,
which is when this book takes place, blacks—or
African Americans—were called "colored."
Then, the black population of Detroit was shut
out of power, whereas today the city has its fourth
black mayor and a mostly black city council.
In 1930, 7 percent of Detroit's population was
black. Today, the 2000 U.S. Census reports Detroit's black population at 82 percent.

Before the start of the Great Depression,
which came in 1929, the city of Detroit experienced a rapid growth in population. Whites and
blacks, especially from the South, came here to
seek jobs and a better way of life in the factories
that made cars and car parts. When the Great
Depression came, jobs became scarce in Detroit
as well as the rest of the country. Most people
struggled to earn a living and care for their families.

In addition, segregation—the separation of the races—was enforced by "Jim Crow" laws in the South. In northern cities like Detroit, segregation was not a matter of law but existed in practice and tradition.

This book takes place in the summer of 1935. It is based on a true story. When I was a little girl, I would sit in my grandparents' yard under the apple, cherry, and peach trees that grew there. I loved to sit under those trees in the summer and listen to my grandparents, my mother, my aunts, and my uncle talk of the Depression era, when instead of trees in the backyard, there was a great big wood yard. This is where my grandfather owned and operated his wood business. This is their story. This is the story they told to me.

1

Wood-Burning Stoves

No fire, no oatmeal. No fire, no oatmeal. No fire
. . . Douglas Ford Jr. repeated the words over
and over in his head.

He was hungry. And the force of those
words—first thing in the morning—was enough
to push him out of bed.

His eyes were still closed. But he did not need
his sight to fold up his cot and push it against
the living-room wall.

The room was cold. But the smell of ashes
made the air seem warm.

He opened his eyes. The room was still dark
as he made his way past the wood-burning stove
in the dining room. His father would soon fill
that stove with heavy pieces of oak. The way his
dad worked a fire, that stove gave off enough
heat to warm the whole front of the house. As
the oldest child—and the only boy—Doug Jr.'s
job was to start the fire in the other stove in the

kitchen. *No fire, no oatmeal.*

Doug Jr.—or Doug, as everyone called him—had started working the wood the night before. The kindling had to be seasoned to make a good fire, so he'd grabbed an armload of sticks from the back porch. Snow had blown onto the porch and onto the sticks, and he'd brushed it off the wood, wrapped the sticks in newspaper, then placed them in the oven when his mother had finished cooking for the day. The oven was just warm enough to season the wood overnight, so the wood got good and dry. *No fire, no oatmeal.*

Cold cereal was what the family ate for breakfast if Doug did not build the fire. He'd slept too long once and didn't make the fire. Then, they had had to eat cold cereal on a cold morning. It never happened again.

The wood was crackling now. He could feel the heat from the stove as it filled the room. "I'll be in to start the oatmeal," his mother called from the bedroom off the kitchen. That's where three of his sisters slept. Doug settled into his chair at the kitchen table. He had done his job.

But before the oatmeal, there was something else. Doug heard the sound of trucks and the smell of exhaust fumes. *The men were coming to work!*

Mr. Jones, Mr. Poniakowski, Mr. Katzinger, Mr. Evert, Mr. Johnson. Colored neighbors, Polish and German neighbors—they all lived up and down Halleck Street. Their pickup trucks pulled into his father's wood yard most mornings. They all worked for his dad, Douglas Ford Sr. They all worked for the Douglas Ford Wood Company.

Doug dug his spoon into his bowl of steaming-hot oatmeal, looking out the kitchen window as he ate. They all tipped their caps to his father as he walked into the yard. Doug knew them all, except one.

His dad talked about him, but Doug never saw his truck. He never came with the other men in the morning. Doug heard his name often enough, so he knew he worked for his dad. But he never saw him.

His name was Jim Hines.

Frostbite

Vroom . . . Vroom . . . Vroom . . . Douglas Ford Jr.
knew the sound of *that* engine. He listened for
it every day after school. Sometimes he hurried
home just to make sure he beat the trucks. Leav-
ing his sisters behind at the playground, he'd
rush home and sit in the living room by the front
door. It was winter. He would have been warmer
sitting in the dining room by the stove in there.
That's where his three sisters sat when they
came home from school. That's where they read
books and played with their dolls and tried to
teach their baby sister Annie May how to walk.
But Doug sat in the living room. He wanted to
hear the hum of the engine of his dad's Model A
pickup truck as he turned from Dequindre Road
onto their street—Halleck Street—and then into
their driveway.

Not that long ago the sound had been different. Then, when his father had turned from the

smooth asphalt-paved Dequindre Road, Halleck Street had been nothing but dirt road and deep ruts. In rainy weather, the weight of the pickup trucks loaded with wood had made the ruts even deeper, and the truck's frame had bounced on its chassis. The sound that rang out was loud and piercing. *Kerchunk. Kerchunk. Kerchunk!*

Sometimes a truck would get stuck in a rut. Doug loved watching the commotion that followed! He would look out the dining-room window as the drivers yelled back and forth.

"Hey, Jones, don't push till I say so!"

"Hold it steady, the wood's ready to give way."

"Katzinger, keep up your end."

Even Pointo, their old hound dog, would yelp from the wood yard and add to the noise.

The drivers would push the truck at the front and the back until it rocked. Sometimes the truck got to rocking so hard Doug thought it would tip over. Sometimes it looked dangerous—when the truck finally got out of the rut, many a time it flew so high that the drivers had to dash to the side or else get run over.

But those days were gone now on Halleck Street. It was 1935 now, and while most of Detroit's streets off the main roads were still gravel and dirt, Halleck Street wasn't like that any-more. Not since his father had changed things.

Douglas Ford Sr. had been a chauffeur and cook in New Orleans, Louisiana, before he moved to Detroit in 1922. As a chauffeur, he'd learned to drive any kind of vehicle. That's why he started a trucking business soon after he'd moved up north—driving was something he loved to do and was good at. But he got sick and tired of the ruts in the road.

So a few years back, he had ordered long, foot-wide planks of lumber. He and his men—even some neighbors that didn't work for him—had laid out the wood over the dirt road. They jammed small wedges of wood between the planks to fit them in tight. Doug's father took the wood down to the end of the block, way past their house. In this way, their street had been "paved." He had paved their driveway too.

That's why when Doug heard men's voices yelling this time, he didn't know what to think. He knew a truck couldn't be stuck in a rut. He jumped up and looked out the living-room win-dow. Halleck Street was empty. Some of the driv-ers were already in the wood yard. His father was barking orders at them—

"Get the wood out of the truck. Pile it up over there! Come on now, move!"

Doug had never heard his father speak to his drivers so harshly. Then he heard a loud squeaking noise. It sounded like the hood of his dad's truck was being raised.

His dad strode into the kitchen through the back door. "May!"

His mother, May Ford, was standing by the sink with the baby girl, Annie May, in her arms.

"Oh my God!" May Ford gasped. His dad's deep, dark-brown skin looked ashen. "Douglas!" His mother always called his dad by his full name.

"Get some towels. Put them on the stove!"

She quickly put the baby in the high chair.

"Daddy!" Doug called out from the living room.

"Do as I say now May. Come on . . ." he said in a pleading voice.

Doug ran into the kitchen. He stood there frozen in his steps.

May Ford peered at her husband's face.

"Frostbite," her husband stated plainly.

"Frostbite?"

Douglas Ford nodded. She looked worried.

"Should I send Doug for Mrs. Barker?" she asked.

"No!" his father answered. "I don't want her in the house. I can't stand the stink of that goose grease she brings with her. That woman thinks it heals everything!"

He pointed over at the stove. "Not too hot, now. Gimme those towels!"

Doug's mother handed her husband the towels. "I know it's still cold out and all. But you were in the truck. How did you get this frostbite?"

He placed the towels across his face. In a muffled voice, he began to explain what happened.

Doug stood over to the side and listened.

"I was at the Durham factory yard. Jones was there with his truck, too. We had just broken up some crates. We were loading some of the wood into my truck."

Douglas Ford Sr. handed his wife one of the towels he had been using to warm his face. She moved quickly and put it back on the stove. He kept talking.

"I didn't see it comin'. One of the switch engines was movin' a car over to another track."

Doug was trying to picture the scene as his

father talked. He had never been to one of the factories with his dad. But he knew enough about the business to know that his dad was talking about a *train* car.

"I just didn't see it comin'. That switch engine knocked my truck clean over! My favorite truck too."

He let his wife put fresh towels on his face.

"All that steam comin' out . . ." He shook his head. "I could tell right away my radiator was busted."

"I'm not worried about the radiator!" May cried out. "You could have been hurt. Killed, for goodness sake!"

"No, May, it's my radiator I'm worried about." He took the towels off of his face.

His face was still ashen. "I still don't know how we got that truck back up. But we did it!"

"Mr. Ford!"

Doug knew that voice. It was Mr. Jones. Because he was a family friend as well as a driver, he was welcome to come into the house.

He took off his hat as he entered the kitchen. He was a big man with a booming voice to match. "Trucks're all unloaded."

Doug's heart sank. His father always let him

help unload his truck before he and the drivers made their deliveries.

Mr. Jones stared at Mr. Ford's face. "Frost-bite?"

"Sure feels like it," Mr. Ford answered.

His wife came over with more towels. He motioned for her to wait. He started barking out more directions to Mr. Jones.

"Listen, now. Get that radiator out and take it to one of the radiator shops up on Joseph Campau Street."

"Does it matter . . ."

"Nope. Any of 'em as long as they can fix my radiator. I just need my truck back."

Mr. Jones nodded his head. He put his hat on as he walked toward the back door.

"Jones!" his father called out.

Mr. Jones turned back around.

"I'm gonna need extra help with my deliveries this evening."

"Sure thing."

"May," Douglas Ford motioned to his wife. "Write down my deliveries for him and the others, the ones I was gonna make this evening."

May Ford grabbed her big ledger from the shelf over the sink. She also took down an inkwell, pen, and paper. She began to write a list of names, addresses, and the amount of money people owed for the wood.

"No, May," he stopped her. "Write each order on a separate piece of paper. Give the double order to Poniakowski." He already knew the stops the drivers had to make that evening. "Evert, Johnson, Katzinger—give them each one extra delivery. Jones, you take the rest."

Mr. Jones looked at the papers she handed him.

"Do you need directions?" she asked.

"Nope. I think we know these streets." He looked at Douglas Ford. "We'll take care of it," he said and walked out the back door.

May Ford put the ledger back on the shelf. "Douglas, you still haven't told me how in heaven's name you got frostbite from all of this," she said.

Doug stepped forward to take a closer look at his dad's face.

Without noticing his son, the father leaned back in his chair. He covered his face with another towel. "That was my favorite truck," he muttered.

"Douglas, tell me!"

"There's not much more to tell, May," he said in a tired voice. "We loaded up the truck and headed back home. The steam was steady comin' out of the radiator. It froze on the windshield—I couldn't see. I had to roll down my side window and stick my head out to drive. So between the steam shootin' out and the cold wind blowin' on my face. . ." His voice trailed off. "There you have it."

"Oh, Douglas," she sighed.

Doug stepped closer to his dad. "I could help you, Dad," he offered.

"You're a big help to me now, son," his father answered.

Doug already helped his dad in the wood yard. He'd been helping him since he was nine years old. He helped when his father returned from his runs to the factories. The auto factories and their suppliers got their deliveries in huge wooden crates. Once they were empty, the crates were of no more use. They were garbage. So the Douglas Ford Wood Company picked up these crates—for free. They broke them down into separate planks right there at the factory yard and then filled up their trucks with wood.

Doug always ran out to the driveway to help

12

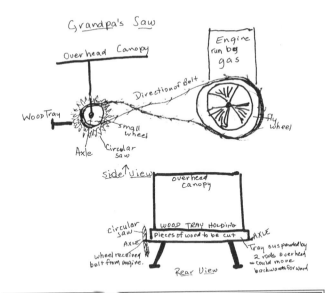

Grandpa's Saw

Overhead Canopy

Engine run by gas

Direction of Belt

Wood Tray

small wheel

Axle

Circular saw

Fly wheel

Side View

overhead canopy

circular saw

WOOD TRAY HOLDING pieces of wood to be cut

AXLE

AXLE

wheel received belt from engine.

Tray suspended by 2 rods overhead or could move backward to forward

Rear View

Sketch of donkey saw with overhead canopy

---

unload his father's truck. He'd have on his work
gloves and his canvas work shoes. He'd grab
as many planks of wood as he could carry. The
other drivers emptied their trucks, too. They'd
pile the wood over by his dad's saw—the donkey
saw. His father would stand at his saw for hours
and cut the planks into pieces small enough to
fit into the wood-burning stoves his customers
used for heating and cooking.

Doug worked hard for his father. Even with the gloves on, he got plenty of splinters in his hands. Some of those splinters were long, and they hurt. Sometimes the planks of wood still had nails in them. Doug stepped on quite a few of those nails. But he never complained, not about the splinters or the nails or working in cold weather. He didn't even mind working in hot weather—in summer, people still needed wood to use for cooking in their kitchen stoves. He'd do anything, anything at all, just to be helping his dad. Just to be a part of his dad's business.

"But Dad," Doug continued, "I could go to the factories with you—"

His mother's back stiffened when she heard what he had in mind. But his dad's body language didn't change.

"That'll come later, son. Later. But I *have* been thinking something else. You're twelve years old now. Maybe you could start helping me with my deliveries. I could get a lot more done if—"

Doug didn't wait for his father to finish what he had to say. "Yes, dad!" He was ecstatic. "I'll do whatever you want!"

"It'll be hard work. Maybe harder than you

realize."

"I can do it, Dad. I know how to work hard. You know that." He straightened his back, stuck out his chest.

"Yes, son. You're a good worker."

"Tomorrow, Dad?"

His father grunted and shifted in his seat. "Can't say when. I'll let you know when. But right now, I've gotta take care of this frostbite."

At that, Doug's mother handed her husband another towel. He put the used one in her other hand.

"Dad—?" He hesitated before asking his question. Instinctively, he knew his dad might not want to answer him.

"What is it, son?"

Doug shifted his feet. "When you gave all of the drivers extra work to do . . ."

"Yes?"

"Well, when you named all the drivers, why did you leave off Jim Hines? You named all of 'em except Jim Hines. Why don't you want him to help you?"

"We'll talk about him another day, but not today," he said, shaking his head beneath the towel. "Not today."

3

Dancing the Polka

Polka, polka, polka! Polka, polka, polka! Their neighbors' whole house seemed to shake. It was Saturday night. The accordion music came from the house next door where the Yablonskis lived.

Doug crouched behind three of his younger sisters—Patsy, Laura, and Jean—as they kneeled at the windowsill in their bedroom. Each one was two years younger and a head shorter than the other. Doug, at twelve, was not only the oldest but also the tallest, so he crouched behind the girls at their bedroom window as they quietly peered into the Yablonski house. The houses in their neighborhood were on small city lots and were built close together. They could see clearly Mr. Yablonski as he sat on a stool in the kitchen playing his accordion—*polka, polka, polka*—and swaying to the beat. *Polka, polka, polka!* All that man played was polkas. Everybody in that house was dancin' the polka. Doug

16

and the girls knew each Saturday night they'd be dancin' the polka. *Polka, polka, polka!* They'd be dancin' the polka all night long.

Doug turned toward the kitchen. "Hey— Mama's dancin'!" he called out to his sisters. "Mama's *dancin'*!"

"She's doin' the polka!" Jean squealed as the four of them rushed into the kitchen. They stood by the stove and stared. They stared at their mother bouncing to the music, lifting her legs to the beat.

"What's wrong with you all? Lookin' like you haven't seen somebody dance a *polka* before . . ."

"Oh, May," their father chuckled, standing in the doorway to the kitchen. He held the baby, Annie May, in his arms.

"Come on," their mother said, grabbing the girls. Patsy and Laura joined her. But Jean pulled away.

"Unh-unh," she said shaking her head.

Doug clapped his hands to the music. His mother and the two older girls danced.

Then Jean asked, "Mama, are you Polish?"

May Ford didn't miss a beat. "You know I'm colored. Just like the rest of you."

"You don't look colored," Jean insisted.

17

Patsy and Laura spoke up almost at the same time while they danced. "Unh-unh, Mama doesn't look like she's Polish," Laura said.

"Mama looks colored . . ." Patsy added.

Jean shook her head. "Daddy looks colored . . ."

Their father's skin was a deep, dark brown.

"Doug and Patsy and Laura and Annie May and me, we look colored . . ."

The children were lighter than their father but still brown-skinned. The color of milk chocolate candy.

"Now, Jean . . ." Douglas Ford began, but his wife cut him off before he could finish talking.

"God makes colored folks all different shades of brown," May Ford answered as she wiped her sweaty face with her apron. She and the two girls had stopped dancing by then.

Doug hadn't said anything. He'd heard that answer before. He'd asked his mother the very same question when he was Jean's age. Now, he just looked at her. She did look white. Even his two best friends teased him about that. He'd almost fought them again about it the day before. "Your mama's white! Your mama's white!" Frankie Jones and Henry Reese laid it on as they walked home after school. Doug had a temper, and his friends knew how to get it flared up. "Your mama's white! Your mama's white!" They kept it up.

Doug had stepped in front of them and pulled back his fist. He was ready to take them both on. Doug looked more like Frankie, who was just a little taller and skinny. Henry was short and squat. It didn't matter which one got it first as far as Doug was concerned. He took aim at Frankie first and yelled at him, "Yeah, well, you gotta limp! Can you run away from this?" Doug knew how to fight back. Frankie's left leg was shorter than the other and he was very self-conscious about the limp.

"OK! OK! I'm sorry," Frankie said, backing off. "Me too," Henry added. Doug didn't believe them, but he put down his fist anyway. He had turned and walked on home ahead of them.

The kids at their school, Jefferson School, were mostly Polish, just like the neighborhood. Doug and his two friends were just about the only colored boys in the seventh grade. There were a few more colored students in his sisters' classes. The teachers had all been white, too, until that year. The colored parents had signed

19

a petition asking for colored teachers. Two had been hired—a librarian and an art teacher.

There were a few other colored neighbors living near the Ford family on Halleck Street. There were some on the streets to the north of Halleck—McLean, Lawley, Dearing, Grant, and Davison—as well on Burnside, McPherson, and Carpenter, the streets to the south. These families came from the southern United States, as had Douglas and May Ford. But most of their neighbors were Polish with a few Germans. In fact, five streets to the east of their house was Joseph Campau Street and the border of the tiny city of Hamtramck, which was almost all Polish. From his front porch, Doug could see his new Eastern European neighbors as they stepped off the Baker streetcar line. His mother had said something about them coming through some-place called Ellis Island in New York. She said they had all of their worldly goods in those big black trunks of theirs. Doug liked to watch as they dragged those trunks down the street.

While most other parts of Detroit were either all colored or all white, whites from Eastern Europe still streamed into Doug's neighborhood even when blacks from the South started mov-

ing in too. Doug did not realize it yet, but such a
racial mixture was rare—very rare—for a neighborhood in Detroit.

Living in the midst of so many Polish neighbors, it started to seem almost natural to Doug
that his mother should look like one of them.
Doug had even picked up a few of their words.
He knew the women tied brightly colored *ba-
bushkas* across their heads. And they ate *paczkis*
the day before Ash Wednesday. And even his
dad liked to walk to the Polish butcher shop
on Joseph Campau Street to buy some of their
dark red *blood sausage.* Doug used to eat blood
sausage. But not anymore—he spit it out of his
mouth, in fact, right back on the plate when his
dad had told him what it was called.

Blood sausage. Not good. Like what had happened earlier that same day. He'd seen a plate of
blood sausage on the kitchen table, then heard a
man outside in the wood yard with a heavy Polish accent say, "T'ank you Mr. Ford. T'ank you."
Doug had looked out the window. He'd never
seen the man before. The man bowed his head
and tipped his hat, then went over to the wood
pile and filled an old wheelbarrow with wood.

Doug had been little when he'd first heard

someone talk like that. His father had explained, "He's from the old country. From Eastern Europe. They talk like that when they first come over here."

Doug kept watching the man. He didn't leave the wood yard after he filled his wheelbarrow; he began moving some planks of wood from one of the trucks over to the donkey saw.

His father came into the house. "Who's that man?" Doug asked him. "Why's he doin' my job?"

"Get away from the window, son."

"But why is he doing *my* job?"

His father sat down at the kitchen table and pulled the plate of blood sausage closer to him. He took the pen knife out of his pocket and began slicing the sausage. "The Depression's hard on folks, son."

The Depression. Doug had heard that word many times before, sometimes when his parents talked, sometimes when some of their neighbors—their colored neighbors—came over to the house on Sundays after dinner for ice cream.

"But that's my job!" Doug raised his voice. He could feel his temper starting to flare up. "You gave that Polish man my job!"

"Now you settle right down, young man," his father said sternly. He pushed the plate away a bit and gestured at Doug with the knife. "That man lives nearby, on Burnside. He's having a bit of hard luck. He can't afford to pay me for the wood, so I give him some work to do. Then he gets to take some wood home for his family."

Doug was still angry. "So why don't you just hire him?" he said with sass in his voice. "Like Mr. Jones and Mr. Katzinger and—"

"Don't smart talk me!" His father cut him off sharply. "Now you know folks need wood to heat their houses and cook their food. I sell them wood, sell it for a fair price. So they like to buy from me. Business is good, even in this Depression. I can hire *some* of our neighbors to help me work the business. But I can't hire everybody."

The next thought just seemed to pop out of nowhere. "He could take the place of Jim Hines," Doug blurted out. "I hear you and Mama talk about him, but I never see him come around here anyway."

His dad shot right back. "Jim Hines works when I need him. He's important to the business. Nobody's gonna take his job."

The polka music stopped, jolting Doug back to

the present. "No more polka," Jean announced from the kitchen. Doug joined the two older girls back at the window. They looked—the stool was empty. "He's gone," Patsy whispered out loud. "No more dancin'."

Laura nodded her head.

"Mr. Yablonski's gone!" Doug called out to the kitchen.

"I guess the party's over early tonight," his mother said. "Just as well."

"Come on, May," his father pleaded. He had a grin on his face. "I'll turn on the radio if you want. I betcha I can find a polka for you. You can keep dancin'."

May Ford ignored the offer. "Come on, children," she said, smiling to herself. "Church tomorrow. It's time for bed."

That night Doug lay on his cot, thinking. He thought about Mr. Yablonski playin' his polkas, about his mother looking Polish, about the Polish man who had taken his job that afternoon. He thought about what his dad had said about Jim Hines. Jim Hines . . .

"If Jim Hines is so important, why hasn't he ever come around the house? Does he live around here? Have I ever seen him? Is he Polish too?" Doug curled up under the covers before dozing off to sleep. "I'll figure it out. I'll figure out who's this guy Jim Hines . . ."

4

Lost Schoolbooks

Vriing-vriing! Vriing-vriing! The time was seven-thirty in the morning. It was the first telephone call of the day. Their mother didn't have to say a word. Her folded arms said it all. Doug and his sisters knew what she was waiting for one of them to do.

Vriing-vriing! Vriing-vriing! Patsy, Laura, and Jean kept eating their hot oatmeal, looking down at their bowls. Baby Annie May fussed in her high chair. Doug saw his mother standing by the phone, her arms still folded across her chest.

Vriing-vriing! Vriing-vriing! Doug sprang out of his seat at the kitchen table. He grabbed Annie May from her high chair, took her to the girls' bedroom off the kitchen, and shut the door. The room was quiet.

Vriing-vriing! May Ford picked up the receiver and spoke into the telephone.

"Douglas Ford Wood Company," she announced pleasantly. "Yes, good morning, Mr. Ludlow. Yes we can. One-half cord of wood. Certainly. This evening. Why thank you, I'll be sure and pass that along."

After hearing the click of the receiver, Doug opened the bedroom door. He brought the baby back into the kitchen.

"Thank you, Doug," his mother said as she took Annie May from his arms and placed her back in the high chair.

"And you girls—" Her voice was not so pleasant now. "Don't wait for your brother to take the baby every time the phone rings!"

"But Mama, Doug was closest to the high chair," Laura protested.

Their father entered the kitchen from the back porch. "Don't argue with your mother!" he demanded. Patsy and Laura jumped in their seats as he scolded them.

"Yes, Daddy," Laura answered softly.

"You know it's good for business for people to think they're calling an office—"

"Yes, Daddy," both Patsy and Laura answered this time.

"—and *not* my kitchen," he finished, and sat down in front of his steaming bowl of oatmeal.

Even so, the telephone on the kitchen wall was not just for the business calls of the Douglas Ford Wood Company. It also happened to be the only phone in any of the neighbors' houses for blocks around the Ford house. So any time of day or night, if there was an emergency—someone needed to call the fire department or call a doctor—there'd be a knock on their door. Colored or white, it didn't matter. Douglas and May Ford never turned anyone away.

Pointo the hound dog started yelping in the yard.

"My drivers must be pulling up," Douglas Ford announced, still eating.

"This morning Mr. Ludlow on Westminster Street called in an order for half a cord of wood," May Ford reported.

"Good customer," he said.

"And he said to please tell Mr. Ford that his colored driver Jim Hines is very polite," she said with a smile.

"I'll be sure and do that—"

Doug perked up. "So Jim Hines is colored?" he asked.

"Who's Jim Hines?" Jean asked, oatmeal still in her mouth.

"Yes, he's colored," their father answered flatly.

"He works for Daddy, doesn't he," Patsy answered.

"Does he have his own truck?" asked Laura.

Then Doug asked, "Does he live around here?"

His father stood up. "Yep. Yep. Yep. Gotta go."

"But where? What street?" Doug pressed on.

His father ignored him. After kissing May on the bun she wore on the back of her head, he was gone out the back door.

Doug sank back in his chair and pouted, "Ma, can *you* tell me about Jim Hines?"

She ignored the question, too. "Hurry on now," she urged the older children. "No time to talk. Eat your food. It's almost eight o'clock. Time to get off to school!"

The dog still yelping, Douglas Ford called out, "Jones, Evert, Poniakowski, let's go! Where are Johnson and Katz? OK, here they come now. Let's head on out!"

———

It would have been a school day like any other

for Doug: Walk the three blocks up Dequindre to Jefferson School. Math, English, and social studies classes in the morning. Home for lunch. Kickball in the playground at recess. Science, Latin, and gym classes in the afternoon. Back home.

But that day at recess, Doug, Frankie, and Henry decided to stop by Shorty's after school. They each had a nickel, and they wanted to buy some candy. Shorty's was a small grocery store a few blocks north of the school on Davison and Goddard. It was owned by a colored man, but there were always both colored and white customers in the store. Doug's mother said he had the freshest vegetables around. Everybody called him Shorty.

Right after school, the three boys headed straight for Shorty's. Doug and Henry walked on either side of Frankie, occasionally imitating him with exaggerated limps as they made their way up Dequindre to Davison. All three had notebooks and schoolbooks tied together and slung across their backs. The only difference was that Doug's parents had bought his books for him. Frankie and Henry—like most of the other youngsters—had to share the books that were provided by the school. Sometimes there were books for them to take home, and sometimes there weren't. But Douglas and May Ford made this promise to all of their children: As long as they did well at school, they would buy them their own books. Education was that important to them. And business at the Douglas Ford Wood Company was going well enough that, even in the midst of the Depression, they could afford to do this for their children.

"A box of punkin' seeds, taffy, licorice . . ." Doug called off as they headed across Davison to Goddard.

"Nah man, I'm gettin' me a caramel on a stick, a box of sprinkles, some chewies, some licorice . . ." Frankie said.

"You can't get all that," Henry interrupted. "Caramel on a stick costs two cents. You only gotta nickel!"

"Yes I can!" Frankie answered. "I'll just get me one of each."

"And chewies are two for a penny," Doug added, backing Frankie up.

A nickel could buy a lot of penny candy.

When they got to Shorty's, they headed straight for the candy counter. They were the first ones there, but other kids from school were close behind them. Doug placed his books on top of the glass counter and peered inside. Candy was piled high. Every kind of candy you could think of. All of his favorites. Shorty himself waited on them. He filled their orders quickly. He even put an extra peppermint candy in each of their bags. They were back out the door in no time.

By the time Doug made it home, he had finished all of his candy, and his stomach hurt. He dragged up the back steps. He could just make out the sound of his mother's voice. She was on the telephone.

"One cord. Yes. We can do that tomorrow. Thank you." She hung up the phone.

Vriing-vriing! Vriing-vriing! May Ford smiled at her son as he walked into the kitchen and sat down at the kitchen table. Patsy, Laura, and Jean were already sitting and eating toast. She spoke quickly. "Orders have been coming in all afternoon," was her only greeting. She picked up the phone. "Douglas Ford Wood Company."

Doug's mother was his father's partner in the business. She placed ads in the newspapers. She answered the telephone. She wrote down the orders for wood. She counted the money. She balanced the books.

But she hadn't always done that. She often told the children about her life before she married their father. She was the teacher in a one-room schoolhouse for the colored children in Clarksville, Tennessee. Then she married their father and moved up to Detroit. But she told them there was something she always regretted—that she hadn't finished that "project" before she got married. She was one "project" away from getting her teaching certificate in home economics at Tennessee State University. Then she could have been one of the colored teachers in Detroit. There weren't many. But she could have been one of them.

That's why she had already started saving for her children's college educations. Doug was going to be a doctor. The girls would be teachers. They would all get their degrees. That was the plan. And they knew it.

"How was school today?" May Ford asked her son.

"OK," he answered. There was chocolate smeared across his cheek.

"I see you've been to Shorty's," she said.

"Mm hmm," Doug answered resting his head on the table.

"Where are your books?" his mother asked.

Doug sat straight up. "Aaah!" he gasped.

"Ooh! Doug's in trouble!" Patsy said.

"Mm hm," Laura added.

"Why?" Jean asked, still eating toast.

"He didn't bring his books home!" Patsy answered.

"Doug? Where did you leave your books? At Shorty's?" his mother asked. "Doug?"

He didn't even answer. He was out the back door and running toward Dequindre.

———

"Your mother told me what happened. Find your books?" Douglas Ford peered over the newspaper from his seat at the kitchen table. Doug was back home.

"No." Doug hung his head. "I'm sorry, Daddy. Mama." He looked over at his mother as she stirred a pot on the stove.

"Son, I know you are." his father said.

His mother kept stirring the pot. She just listened.

34

His dad continued. "You made a mistake and this is a hard lesson for you. I want you have fun with your friends. But you can't be careless."

"Yes, sir."

"You'll get new books—"

"Thanks, Daddy!" Doug interrupted. His face brightened.

"Now listen to me," his father cautioned. "We can get you more books easy enough. That's not a problem. But we think it would be better for you if you earned the money yourself to pay for the books."

"Oh, OK," Doug answered. He looked downcast again. He wondered to himself how he was ever going to make enough money to do that. Cutting grass for neighbors, maybe. Running errands . . .

"And you'll do it by working for me. You'll start making deliveries with me today," his father added.

"Today? Yes, sir!" Doug was shocked. He couldn't believe it. While he still felt bad about losing the books at Shorty's, he was head-over-heels happy at the thought of going out in the truck with his Dad. Working with his dad as part of the crew. Working like Mr. Evert, Mr. Jones,

Mr. Katzinger . . . Only he'd be Douglas Ford Jr. of the Douglas Ford Wood Company! "And who knows?" he thought to himself. "I just might get to meet ol' Mr. Jim Hines!"

"Now go change into your work clothes," his mother spoke up.

"And meet me in the yard in ten minutes," his father added.

5

Delivering Wood

Kuurlunk, kuurlunk, kuurlunk . . . Kuurlunk, kuurlunk, kuurlunk.

He wasn't expecting there to be so much noise. *Kuurlunk, kuurlunk, kuurlunk.* It made his ears ring. *Kuurlunk, kuurlunk, kuurlunk.* That was the sound of the wood from his dad's wheelbarrow going down the chute to a customer's basement. If the customer didn't have a driveway, Doug got paid seventy-five cents to cart the wood from the curb to the chute at the side of the house. His father unloaded the wood at the curb, and he left Doug with the wheelbarrow, a broom, and a shovel while he went on and delivered the next order. Then he'd swing back around and pick up Doug.

Kuurlunk, kuurlunk, kuurlunk. Kuurlunk, kuurlunk, kuurlunk.

When a customer's house did have a driveway, Doug's dad pulled the truck right up beside the house. Then, Doug got paid twenty-five cents to unload the wood straight from the truck to the chute. But it was the same noise. *Kuurlunk, kuurlunk, kuurlunk.*

He'd been working for his dad a couple of weeks now, and it hadn't taken Doug long to figure out why he got paid so much more when he had to load up the wheelbarrow at the curb—it was the pain. He hadn't expected the pain. *Kuurlunk, kuurlunk, kuurlunk. Kuurlunk, kuurlunk, kuurlunk.* Hauling that wheelbarrow made him ache up and down his spine. The splinters and blisters on his hands were nothing compared to that low, dull ache he felt as he stooped over trying to balance the load up to the house. The sawdust caked in his nose was nothing compared to the sharp cramp in his back as he tried to straighten up again. Doug had no idea there would be the noise . . . and the pain. Those things were a big surprise all right. But they weren't the only surprises.

Doug thought back to his first day of making deliveries with his dad. Douglas Ford had climbed in the driver's seat and started the engine. Doug climbed in on the passenger side.

"Are you ready, son?" his father asked him.

"Yes, Daddy, I'm ready!"

"Wave to your mother," he told him.

Doug looked over to the kitchen window and waved. His mother was standing there, holding baby Annie May. Laura, Patsy, and Jean giggled in the window as they waved and made faces at him.

"Then let's get going!" his father charged.

And they were off.

Doug watched his father drive. He noticed when his dad lifted his foot off the clutch and when he pressed down. He studied him when he shifted gears and when he put his arm out to signal a turn. They didn't talk much.

Then Doug broke the silence. "Where's our first stop? When're we gonna get there, Dad?" he asked.

"Not much longer," his father answered. "We'll start in Grosse Pointe this trip," he explained.

Doug smiled and sat up straight. "I can't wait to tell them that I'm Douglas Ford Jr. of the Douglas Ford Wood Company!" he exclaimed. He rubbed his hands together. "I've been waitin' a mighty long time for this—"

"You won't need to talk to anybody," his father

replied plainly.

"What?" Doug asked.

"In fact, they probably won't say anything to you."

"Really? But I thought . . ."

"The only one they'll need to talk to is me when I go to collect what they owe me for the wood."

"Oh," Doug responded sadly. He slumped back in his seat. That was the first surprise. "What's the use of having my dad's name on the business if nobody's gonna know I'm his son?" he asked himself.

It was a long ride. They took Davison to Mound Road to Jefferson. His dad pointed out some of the big streets—Cadieux, Moross, Kercheval. Douglas Ford didn't say much else. It seemed to Doug they just kept on going . . . driving and driving . . .

And then he noticed something while his dad was driving. All of a sudden he saw it. It was the next surprise—the people were all white. Walking on the streets, coming out of stores. They were all white. And for the first time in his life, he realized that there were places where there weren't any colored people. These places weren't like his neighborhood, with colored and white living together. Even in Hamtramck, with all the Polish people that lived there, he saw colored folks walking up and down Joseph Campau Street. He'd even been to places that were all colored, like the part of Detroit they called Black Bottom. But here was something different. Doug and his father had crossed over into an all-white world.

"Here's the first stop," his father said.

Doug jumped in his seat. "We're there? We made it?"

His dad chuckled. They both hopped out of the truck.

"Here's what you do," Douglas Ford explained. He told Doug about the wheelbarrow, showed him how to open the chute and drop in the wood.

"Then you take this broom and shovel and clean up all the sawdust when you're through. I'll come back and collect the money. Got that?"

"Yes, Daddy," Doug replied.

"You ready?" his father asked.

Doug's face brightened. "Yes, Dad!"

The work sounded easy to Doug. But it was harder and more painful than he ever imagined.

And his dad was right. Nobody spoke to him while he worked. Sometimes he saw a curtain move, but he never saw anybody. And that was another surprise: It was lonely work. His father didn't talk much. None of the customers spoke to him. He thought he'd at least see some of the other drivers on the road. Unh-unh. He never saw any of them. He thought he'd see Mr. Evert turning a corner or Mr. Poniakowski coming down the other side of the road. Never. None of 'em. And if he didn't see any of those guys, he figured he'd never get to meet the one he wanted to see most of all—Jim Hines.

"Why?" he wondered. "Why all the surprises? Why is nothin' like I thought it would be goin' out in the truck with Dad? I didn't even get to see Jim Hines." Then Doug laughed as he thought to himself, "Maybe Dad and Ma are just foolin' me, like with Santa Claus and the tooth fairy. Maybe there really isn't any Jim Hines!"

"Here, son," Douglas Ford said as he got back in the truck and nudged his boy. He handed him something wrapped in newspaper. "That last customer, Mrs. Mann, saw you sitting out in the truck and sent this for you."

Doug quickly tore open the paper. It was a

jelly sandwich made with thick slices of brown bread. He took a bite. He had to cup one hand under the bread so the jelly wouldn't drip onto his overalls. He licked his fingers. The jelly on his fingers tasted like sawdust, but he didn't care. The bread was warm. The sandwich was delicious. He finished it before they got back home.

That first evening when they returned home from making deliveries, Douglas Ford walked quickly into the house through the back door. Doug dragged in behind him. He could barely stand up straight. There was sawdust all over his overalls.

May Ford took one look at her son and scolded her husband. "Douglas, you worked him too hard! Look at him!"

"Oh, May," he defended himself, "the boy'll be all right."

"I hope so," she said as she hugged Doug. "Go wash up," she told both of them. "Dinner's about ready."

Douglas Ford Sr. in chauffeur's uniform,
New Orleans, Louisiana, 1922

Mr. and Mrs. Douglas Ford Sr.
with Douglas Ford Jr., 1925

Douglas Ford Sr. next to company truck

Maber Ford (Mrs. Douglas Ford Sr.) at wood yard
with oldest daughter, Maber, ca. 1929

Douglas Ford Sr. at wood yard holding oldest daughter,
Maber, ca. 1927

Douglas Ford Jr. wearing drum and bugle corps
uniform, holding bugle in right hand

Douglas Ford Sr. next to company truck

Douglas Ford Jr. with parents Mr. and Mrs. Douglas Ford Sr., graduation day, Meharry Medical School, 1951

Ford family residence, 1950 Halleck Street

6

Donkey Saw

Hee haw donkey saw! Hee haw donkey saw! Doug heard the noise loud and clear as he walked home from school with his buddies Henry Reese and Frankie Jones. *Hee haw donkey saw! Hee haw donkey saw!* That's how it sounded to Doug as the saw blade cut through the wood. That was the sound of his dad at the saw in the afternoon after he'd brought in truckloads of wood from the factories. That was the sound of his dad at the saw once deliveries were finished. The pile of wood behind him grew taller and wider as he worked late into the evening. *Hee haw donkey saw! Hee haw donkey saw!*

"Wanna play ball with us?" Henry asked Doug as the three buddies walked home from school and turned onto Halleck Street.

"Nope, not today," Doug answered. "My dad probably wants me to help him with deliveries," he added proudly. "I told ya guys I've been ridin' in the truck with him after school."

"You've been ridin', but have you been *working*?" Frankie asked. He and Henry burst out laughing.

Doug tried to tell them how hard the work was. He opened his hands to show off his thick calluses, but his friends weren't paying any attention. They were busy laughing and pushing at each other as they made their way down the street.

When the boys reached the driveway, all three ran up to where Douglas Ford stood behind his saw. "Step back, boys!" Mr. Ford ordered loudly. His voice carried above the noise of the saw. The boys jumped back. They watched for a minute. Then Henry and Frankie turned and ran down the driveway.

"We're gonna go play some ball! See ya Doug," Frankie yelled over his shoulder.

After Doug watched them leave, he turned and stepped toward his father.

"Get back, son," his father warned. "You know this is dangerous work."

"But Dad, it doesn't look so dangerous," Doug protested.

"No arguments!" he snapped back.

They were both silent for a moment. Then his father began, "This old donkey engine may sound loud and run slow, just like a donkey. But believe you me, it can move this saw. That's why loggers use a donkey engine when they're cuttin' down trees. This saw here can cut through the hardest wood . . . *and* it could cut off a finger." He kept his eyes on the saw while he talked. He used a steady motion, pushing the wood through piece by piece.

"Now, I could keep working if I lost a finger—but you're gonna be a doctor, son. And a doctor needs *all* his fingers," his father cautioned. "You get what I'm sayin'?"

"Yes, sir," Doug replied quietly. He saw Pointo over in a corner of the yard.

"C'mere, doggie!" he called. Then he whistled. The dog came running over. They played fetch with an old chewed-up piece of wood.

Then he asked, "Hey Dad, when're we gonna start loadin' the truck?"

"Not today, son," he answered. "The other trucks'll make all the deliveries today. They're already out now."

"Aww, Dad," he protested.

"You've been out enough this week," his father said, still steady at the saw. "Anyway, I think your mother wants you to go with her and the girls to the post office."

Doug sulked. When he was younger, walking up Joseph Campau Street to the post office in Hamtramck had been a big deal. Now, he thought, "I'd rather be playin' ball with Henry and Frankie."

His mother stood at the door. "We're going to the post office today, Doug. Come in and count your money. You can put it in your account."

He had an account at the post office. From the time they were born, May Ford had opened savings accounts for Doug, Patsy, Laura, Jean, and now Annie May. She put money in each of their accounts every week. "For your college tuition," she told them. Doug would study to be a doctor. The girls would be teachers. There was an account for the business, too. She never missed a week.

"*All* of it?" Doug asked his mother. But he already knew the answer to that one. He knew he had to save everything he earned from the delivery runs until he'd paid his parents back for the new set of school books.

She nodded her head and went back in the

house. Doug followed.

Doug sat at the dining-room table counting his money. The girls were at the table with him, combing their dolls' hair. His mother was in the kitchen. Then the saw stopped running. Doug heard his father enter the kitchen. His parents were whispering. Doug strained to hear. He could barely make it out. "Jim Hines," he heard.

"Jim Hines almost cussed someone out at the factory today," he heard his father say. Then his parents went into the girls' bedroom and shut the door. Doug couldn't hear much more sitting where he was in the dining room, so he snuck up outside the bedroom door in the kitchen. He could make out the words "foreman" and "gate." Then he ran back to the dining-room table.

"This guy Jim Hines is gonna make trouble for Daddy," Doug whispered to his sisters. But they didn't even look up from their dolls. Patsy just shrugged her shoulders.

His father came out of the bedroom and went back outside. Then a moment later—*Hee haw donkey saw! Hee haw donkey saw!*—he was back to cutting wood.

His mother was back in the kitchen. "We're going now!" she called out. "Doug, put your money in your pocket. Everybody get your coats on!"

Doug and the girls scrambled to get ready. Doug stuffed his money deep in his pockets, then got his coat. The girls ran to the hooks by the back door—"No running in the house," their mother reminded them—and got their coats. After she got baby Annie May ready, they followed her outside.

Douglas Ford had stopped running the saw. He was taking the belt from around the fly wheel on the saw. "I think I'll walk down to Joseph Campau with you," he announced to his wife. "This belt is pretty frayed. I'm gonna see if I can't get a new one." He put the belt in his coat pocket and held the stroller still while May Ford buckled Annie May in. Then the whole family headed off down Halleck Street toward Joseph Campau.

The Ford family walking across Halleck to Joseph Campau Street was a familiar sight to all the neighbors. Colored, Polish, German, Lithuanian—everyone knew them. Douglas and May Ford exchanged greetings with any neighbors who happened to be outside.

Henry and Frankie were playing catch on the

sidewalk with some other boys. Doug said hey but kept on walking with his family.

When they turned onto Joseph Campau Street, Douglas stopped at the truck repair shop. It was big and noisy and looked dark inside. "This is where I'll get my belt," he said to May. "Mind your mother," he warned the children and walked inside.

May Ford kept walking with the children, heading straight for the post office.

Inside, she had the girls stand to the side with Annie May in the stroller. "Watch the baby," she instructed them. "Come with me, Doug," she said. She walked with Doug to wait their turn. It was a long line, but it moved quickly. The clerks all knew Mrs. Ford, so when they got to the window, Doug and his mother were finished in no time.

Outside, she bought each of them a piece of licorice candy from a street vendor. Then they headed on back home.

Hee haw donkey saw! Hee haw donkey saw! They could hear the sound of the saw in the wood yard as they walked down Halleck Street. That meant they were close to home. "That's Daddy workin'," Doug said out loud.

Hee haw donkey saw! Heeeraw—the sound ended abruptly.

It sounded funny to Doug. He looked at his mother. She had a puzzled look on her face. They kept on walking. But his mother stepped more quickly behind the stroller.

When they turned into their driveway Douglas Ford was nowhere in sight. They walked farther in and they saw blood. There was blood all over the wood tray by the saw. Blood on the wood planks beneath the saw.

Jean, Laura, Patsy—they all screamed at the sight of it. Pointo started barking back by the fence. Annie May got frightened from all the noise and started wailing in her stroller.

"Jesus Christ!" their mother cried out.

Doug had never heard his mother talk like that.

"Douglas? Douglas? Where are you?" she called out frantically, looking around the wood yard.

The girls had started running toward the back door.

"Come back, girls, and get the baby out of the stroller," their mother ordered.

They turned around. Patsy picked up Annie

May, who was still crying.

Just then, their father came out of the house. His left hand was wrapped in a white cloth. Blood was soaking through.

"Daddy, what happened?" Doug asked as he ran toward him.

May Ford reached him first.

"I knew that saw sounded funny when we were walking down the street. *Now you tell me what happened!*" she demanded.

He held the wrapped hand cupped in his right hand. He sat down on the back steps.

"I knew that belt was too loose when I put it back on the fly wheel. It didn't fit quite right," he explained. "But I kept on working. It was goin' OK. Then the belt snapped loose. The saw blade slipped over. Next thing I know most of the top half of my index finger was pretty near cut off—"

"Oh, Douglas!" his wife cried.

"Blood all over the place," he finished. He shook his head slowly.

The children looked on silently. Even the baby was quiet now. But there was a look of terror in the older ones' eyes as they stood there.

"I rang up Dr. Hammonds. He told me to get to the hospital—City General. I gotta go. Gotta get going *now* so they can sew this finger back on," he announced. He slowly lifted himself up from the steps.

Doug knew Dr. Hammonds. He was the only colored doctor in that part of the city. His office was on Dequindre just east of Davison. Doug also knew that Dr. Hammonds couldn't work out of City General. His mother explained to the children that colored doctors were not allowed to work in the city hospital. "Discrimination," she called it. "Segregation," his father added.

There was a private colored hospital for the colored doctors. But it was crowded—a small space with too many patients. It didn't have the money for all of the equipment City General had, either.

"You need someone else to drive you," his wife said firmly.

"There's no one else around. I'll drive myself."

"Jones or one of the other drivers will be back soon," she responded.

"I can't wait for them. I gotta get over there now. I'll be all right. I can drive with one hand."

"Well, I'm calling the hospital to tell them you're on the way," she said.

Doug watched as his mother hurried up the

back steps into the house.

"You children get on inside. I'll be fine," their father said.

They obeyed and went in the house.

Doug stood at the kitchen window and watched his father grab hold of the truck door handle and pull himself up behind the steering wheel with his one good hand. He rushed to the living-room window and watched his dad drive down the street. In his head he pictured the donkey saw, the loose belt, the blood. He pictured his dad driving up to City General and the doctors unwrapping the cloth from around his hand. White doctors . . .

Doug imagined himself as a doctor, Dr. Douglas Ford Jr., sending his patient with a cut hand to the hospital. Would it be City General or the colored hospital?

"Ham sandwiches!" Jean squealed in the kitchen. Doug quit his daydreaming and joined the girls at the kitchen table. Their mother was slicing the ham she had taken out of the ice box. She took bread, onions, and mustard from the pantry. She cut the bread thick and the onions thin. She spread the mustard on heavy. There were smiles all around as she served the sandwiches. Mustard oozed between their fingers and down their chins as they ate. Even Annie May pushed some bits of ham into her mouth. Ham sandwiches for supper was a real treat.

Vriing-vriing! Doug's mother picked up the telephone right away. He could tell she was talking to someone from the hospital.

She hung up. "That was your father's nurse. They were able to sew the finger back on. Your father's resting now. He'll be home later tonight."

"Yay! Daddy's comin' home!" Doug and the girls shouted. They were out of their chairs and jumping up and down. Annie May clapped her hands from her high chair. May Ford reached out and hugged them all.

Then she said, "Now scoot! Bedtime! You can see your father in the morning."

The girls brushed their teeth and put on their pajamas. They giggled in the bedroom until they fell asleep. Doug unfolded his cot, but he didn't lie down. He sat and waited by the living-room window.

He dozed off. He didn't hear his dad's truck when it pulled up. What he heard was his parents whispering in the kitchen.

"See, May," he heard his father say. "It doesn't look so bad."

"Daddy's home," he said and shook himself awake. "Daddy!" he called out as he ran into the kitchen.

"Shhh," his mother whispered. "Don't wake the girls."

Doug wrapped his arms around his father's waist and hugged him tight.

"Can I see, Daddy? Let me see."

His father held out his left hand. The palm of his hand was caked with blood. There was string sewn all around the index finger. Then the finger was tied to a splint. The other fingers looked bruised.

"Doesn't look so bad, does it, son?"

"No Daddy," Doug answered.

But it did look bad. Doug went to bed that night wondering how that accident had happened. His father was always so careful. What went wrong? Did it have to do with Jim Hines causing trouble at the factory that day? Was he thinking about Jim Hines instead of watching the saw? Would his father ever be able to cut wood again?

Within a few days, Doug was walking home

from school with Henry and Frankie when he heard that sound again—*Hee haw donkey saw! Hee haw donkey saw!* His dad was back at work. He left his buddies behind and ran home.

"Daddy!" he called as he ran up the driveway.

"Stay back, son," was all his father said, not looking up from the saw. "A doctor needs all his fingers."

Wood and Toys

*Vrooommm . . . Vrooommm . . . Vrooommm
. . .* Doug and Henry revved the engines of
their scooters. They stood at the start of the
wood-yard driveway and impatiently waited for
Frankie—standing at the other end—to give the
signal that would start the race.

"C'mon, Frankie! Let's get the race started!"
Doug said, begging his friend.

Frankie laughed. "What's the rush? Henry's
gonna win anyway!" He lowered his white handkerchief. The two friends sped off.

Doug and Henry clutched the wooden han-
dles of their scooters with all their might. With
one foot they pushed their makeshift machines
faster and faster up the driveway while the other
foot barely touched the footboard.

Doug crossed the finish line, crudely marked
with a piece of chalk, before Henry. But Frankie
declared Henry the winner.

"Uh-uh! You know I won! You always say it's Henry!" Doug yelled at Frankie. He threw down his scooter. The wheels, from old roller skates, were still spinning.

"Henry won fair and square," asserted Frankie.

Henry stood to the side, grinning.

"OK, I tell you what," Doug stated. By now he and Frankie were standing nose to nose. "*I'll* be the judge next time. You against Henry," he said. "*Then* we'll see who wins!"

"You're on!" Frankie agreed. He stepped back and grabbed his scooter. "C'mon, Henry."

The two boys trudged back to the start of the driveway with their scooters. Doug took his handkerchief from his pocket, but just as he was about to signal the beginning of the race, he heard the familiar sound of his father's truck. On top of that was the honk of the truck horn. It was the signal for any children playing outside to clear the driveway.

"Outta the way, you guys!" Doug shouted to his friends. "My dad's comin' down the street. Get outta the way!"

Henry and Frankie picked up their scooters and clumsily ran with them to the top of the driveway. They knew to move quickly. No more racing once the trucks were back at the wood yard.

Doug waved as his father parked his truck.

"Hi, Dad! Any good wood today?" Doug ran up and greeted his dad as he stepped out of the truck.

Sometimes his father brought home special pieces of wood from the factories. It was wood that had been used to make small-scale car models. Any scraps or extra pieces were thrown away with the wooden crates. His dad brought them home. They could be in the shape of a wheel, or a door, or a hood, any part of the body of a car. Doug and his friends could make scooters with the wood scraps that they usually found in the wood yard. But they could make even fancier toys—like wagons and box carts—with the special pieces.

"Well, let's see, son," his father answered with a grin. He reached back into his truck. He pulled out an armful of small-scale model wheels.

The boys let out a whoop as they ran up and started grabbing the wheels.

"Use these with the boards I brought home the other day. I think you could make a mighty fine wagon, don't you?" his dad asked with a grin. The boys got busy loading their arms up with wheels.

"And Doug, deliveries in a little while," his father reminded him.

"Yes, Dad," he answered. But he was already walking away with his friends.

Doug, Frankie, and Henry forgot all about their disagreement. They took the wheels over to the box Doug's dad kept by the back steps. It was full of old tools and cast-off machine parts. They pulled out the hammer, then looked for old nails. They searched for rods to use as axles.

Gathering most of what they needed in a pile, Doug said, "Tomorrow's Saturday. You guys come by in the morning—we'll get started on this wagon. I bet it won't take us long."

And it didn't. They finished the wagon by mid-afternoon the next day. "Nobody at school's gonna have a wagon like this!" Doug said proudly. "Nobody!"

"Oooh weee!" Frankie exclaimed. "Just let Johnny Hightower get a look at this. Or Marty or Chester Higgins . . ."

Suddenly a thought came to Doug. He interrupted his friend, blurting out—"You or Henry know anybody last name Hines?"

"Who?" Frankie asked.

"Hines. Know anybody with that last name?"

"Sure I do," Henry remarked.

"Who?" Doug pressed him.

"Charlie Hines. He's in the sixth grade. You know him, don't you, Frankie."

"Nah, not me," Frankie said.

"Show him to me at recess," Doug said. "Is he colored?" he added.

"Yep," Henry answered.

"That's gotta be him!"

"Gotta be who?" Henry asked.

"Just point him out to me on Monday," Doug said.

Doug's heart was racing now. He was getting closer. He could feel it. He was going to meet Charlie Hines. That had to be Jim Hines's boy. And somehow, some way, he was going to work it so that he would finally see—maybe even meet—Jim Hines!

Recess didn't come fast enough for Doug that Monday. He almost pushed his buddies onto the playground after lunch and practically ordered Henry to start looking for Charlie Hines. There was a group of boys over in a corner playing kickball. Henry squinted his eyes and stared over that way.

"There he is! There's Charlie Hines," Henry announced.

"Which one?" Doug asked.

Henry pointed. "Brown shirt. Black cap. See him?"

"Yep, I see him," Doug answered and darted toward the boy. He ran right in the middle of the kickball game.

"Charlie? Are you Charlie Hines?" he asked when he reached him, a little out of breath.

Some of the kids yelled for Doug to get out of the way or play. Doug repeated his question to the boy, who was nodding his head.

"C'mere a minute," Doug said. The boy joined him over at the sideline. "Charlie?"

"Uh huh," the boy said looking over his shoulder at his buddies.

"I'm Doug. Doug Ford. And I was wonderin' something."

Charlie kept glancing over at the game.

"Is your father's name Jim?"

"Why you askin'?"

"'Cause my dad's gotta man workin' for him. Name is Jim Hines. I thought maybe it was your father."

"Nah. My dad's name is Charlie. Like me. But I gotta Uncle Jimmy though."

"You do?" Doug couldn't believe what he was hearing. "Does he work for the Douglas Ford Wood Company?"

"Nah. He lives down South. And it's Himes. The last name is Himes with a *m*. Not Hines."

"But you said . . ."

"Everybody says it wrong. Figured it didn't matter."

Doug kicked the dirt. "Shoot!" he yelled out. He had come so close. "Shoot! Shoot! Shoot . . . shoot . . . shoot!"

"C'mon, Charlie!" somebody called.

Charlie ran back to the game.

Doug kicked the dirt again and again until there was a cloud of dust blowing around him. Then the school bell rang and recess was over.

Doug was still fuming when he got home that afternoon. He didn't even go in the house. He laid his books on the back steps and stayed out in the yard, playing fetch with Pointo. Out of the corner of his eye he saw a board move—one of the loose boards along the back fence. He saw a hand pull the board to one side. A boy, a Polish kid Doug had seen before, squeezed his head and shoulder through and looked around the yard. He grabbed some pieces of wood, as much as he could in one hand. Then he saw Doug. He started to pull himself back out, but his shirt got caught on the board. He tugged and pulled.

In the meantime, Doug pulled back another loose board that was on a different part of the fence and squeezed out into the alley.

"I gotcha! Stealin' my daddy's wood!" Doug grabbed the boy by the legs and pulled at him. "Put the wood back!" he ordered.

"No! Leave me alone!" the boy yelled back.

Doug pulled harder. The boy's shirt ripped.

"Look what you did to my shirt! Let go o' me!"

The boys tussled in the dirt. Doug grabbed for the wood in the boy's hand. He wouldn't let go.

"Gimme my daddy's wood!"

Doug stayed on top of the boy. They fought and hit and spit and hit. Neither one heard Douglas Ford as he stopped his truck at the end of the alley. They didn't hear him running across the dirt.

But Doug did feel his dad's massive hands grab his legs and pull him off the boy.

"Doug, what's going on here?" He pulled Doug up and shook him hard.

"Daddy, he's stealing your wood! I'm tryin' to stop him!" Doug wailed.

"Go on, now!" Douglas Ford ordered the boy. The kid got up and sped down the alley.

"Good thing I was going down Dequindre when I did. What's gotten into you, son?" his father demanded.

Doug was silent.

"I'm talking to you. I expect an answer," his father said firmly.

"Daddy, he was takin' your wood." Doug was almost in tears.

"He's taken it before. I've seen him. Him and a whole lotta other kids from around here. Polish kids like this one, colored kids . . ." Mr. Ford replied. "I see them sometimes in the evenings when I'm workin' my saw."

"Don't you care, Daddy?"

"They don't take that much. And they're just doin' what you and Henry and Frankie do: making toys, scooters, somethin' to play with."

"Then why don't they just ask you for some?"

"That I don't know, son," Douglas Ford replied.

"But that's stealin' though," Doug said. Tears streamed down his face.

"It is. But I guess I don't mind them takin' a bit of wood to make a little somethin' to play with."

Doug just whimpered as the tears rolled down his cheeks.

"Times are tight," his father added as he led his son down the alley toward the truck. "Without that wood, some of 'em might not have any toys at all."

8

Ice Cream Machine

Whirraank! Whirraank! Whirraank! Doug sat alone in the yard behind the house. It was Easter Sunday. He was still wearing his new suit as he sat in the backyard in the worn wood chair he had dragged down from the back porch, turning the crank to the ice cream machine. Things had settled down. There wasn't the noise of a crowded church on Easter Sunday. There wasn't the loud chatter of the family enjoying the Easter feast his mother had worked all weekend to prepare: baked ham, candied sweet potatoes, macaroni and cheese, string beans, buttermilk biscuits. There was just the sound of the turning crank.

Whirraank! Whirraank! Whirraank! Doug kept turning the crank. It was a little harder to move, but he knew that the ice cream was nowhere near ready yet. Then he heard another noise in the yard. Maybe it was Patsy or Laura sneaking up behind him coming to take their turn at the crank. He looked around. It wasn't them. No one was there.

He heard the noise again. He swung his head around in time to see one of the loose boards in the back fence move. "I betcha it's that boy from the other block," he muttered. His arm was getting tired, but not so tired that he couldn't fight. "This time I'll make sure he doesn't come back!"

Then he heard laughter from behind the back fence. "Is it ready yet?" someone asked, trying to disguise his voice to sound like a girl. It didn't take long for Doug to figure out that it was either Frankie or Henry.

One of them pushed the loose board to one side and stuck his head through. "Well," he asked, "is it ready?"

It was Frankie.

"Why don't you come turn this thing and find out for yourself?" Doug answered.

"No, man. That's too much work!

"Move, Frankie!" Henry gave him a little shove and then stuck his own head through the opening. "Can we come back and have some ice cream?"

"Only if you help," Doug answered, steadily

turning the crank.

"Unh-unh. Too much work. Forget it!" Henry declared.

Ri-i-i-i-p!

Henry pulled his head back. "Uh-oh, Frank. Now you gone and done it!"

"My new suit—caught on this nail over here." Frankie wailed.

Henry stuck his head back in the yard. "You should see this tear, Doug. It's big. *Real* big!"

"Ah, man!" Frankie exclaimed from behind the fence. "My mama's gonna kill me! My new Easter suit! I only just wore it today." His voice trailed off as he limped down the alley.

"See ya, Doug," Henry called out as he followed his friend.

Whirraank! Whirraank! Whirraank! Doug's arms were starting to ache. "This is too much for one person," Doug moaned out loud. He stopped turning for a minute and shook out his arms.

The crank turned the dasher that spun the creamy, sweet custard around and around inside a big metal canister. Doug had watched as his father put that huge container inside what was really just a tall bucket. Then, his dad had packed lots of ice chunks and rock salt inside the bucket and around the canister. Because it was a nice day, his father took the whole thing outside like they did in the summer. And there Doug sat—by himself, hunched over the bucket, thinking about holding a big bowl filled with ice cream, turning and turning the crank . . .

Whirraank! Whirraank! Doug knew it was a good thing when the crank was harder to turn. That meant that the custard was freezing. The ice and rock salt were doing their job.

Whirraank! Whirraank! Now the muscle in his shoulder burned. He could barely turn the crank anymore. Then—*Whirraank! Whirr*—the crank stuck. It wouldn't budge. He felt a hand on his shoulder and swung around.

"Oh, Daddy," Doug greeted his father. His voice was weak. He slumped back in the chair.

"Well, son," his dad said smiling down on him, "looks like you finished making that whole bucket full of ice cream by yourself."

"Yeah. Looks like it, Daddy. *Feels* like it too," Doug added weakly, rubbing his arm.

"That was quite a job—good work!" His father reached in his pocket. "Here son. This is for you."

80

It was a quarter. Doug broke into a wide grin.

"Now go help your mother bring out the bowls. Tell her ice cream's ready!"

"Yes, sir!"

As Doug ran into the house, he looked down the driveway and saw that Sunday guests had already arrived. Huddled together by the start of the driveway were their colored neighbors Mr. Chambers, Mr. Clark, Mr. Johnson, and Mr. Jones. Mr. Jones was also one of his dad's drivers. If their wives came, they'd be in the house with his mother.

Doug's family had guests most Sundays. Sometimes they came by to use the telephone. But they always arrived late enough in the afternoon to be offered a bowl of homemade ice cream. They'd eat their ice cream slowly and talk far into the evening. It seemed to Doug that they always talked about important things.

Doug followed his mother back outside, his arms full of bowls and spoons. She sat down in the chair by the bucket. She had a large scoop in her hand.

"Girls!" May Ford called out. "Patsy, Laura, Jean! Come on outside—come and get your dessert!"

She always made sure the children had their ice cream before any guests were served. The men understood this and continued to talk as they stood to themselves. It was also understood that there was never to be any liquor served or drunk at the Ford home. But they were free to light up their cigars. That's why there was a haze of smoke hovering over their heads as they puffed away. Mr. Jones even knew how to blow smoke rings. Doug stood and stared as he watched him tilt his head back and send circles of smoke into the air.

"Here, Doug," his mother nudged him. "Take this bowl of ice cream inside to Mrs. Clark. And tell your sisters to hurry up. I'm not going to wait all evening."

Patsy, Laura, and Jean trailed behind him when he came back out. They were quiet.

"What's the matter with you girls?" May Ford asked as they lined up beside her, still not saying a word. "You feel bad that you didn't help your brother with the ice cream this afternoon? Hm-mmm? Is that why you took so long to come out and get yours? Is that why you girls are so quiet now?"

"But Doug didn't ask us to help," Patsy explained in a low voice.

"He shouldn't have to ask for help. You know we make ice cream every Sunday," their mother replied.

She spoke sternly as she looked each girl square in the eye. "Don't let it happen again. You help your brother next time."

"Yes, Mama," the three girls each answered their mother.

She handed them their bowls, each with a scoop of ice cream. "Now scoot!" They hurried off back into the house to eat at the kitchen table.

"And Doug, *this* is for all your work!"

Doug's face broke into a broad grin as she handed him a bowl almost overflowing with ice cream. "Enjoy your dessert, son," she said, smiling. He took it over by the side of the house, opposite to where the men stood. He sat down on the ground.

After she served the men, May Ford left them to their talk.

It was union talk. That was the word Doug heard over and over again—*union*. The men talked about workers joining to get better pay and better working conditions.

"I'll believe it when I see it," his father said.

"I'm telling you," Mr. Clark said. "I believe it. Times are changin'. At least they are with some of the new unions. I've been hearing a lot of talk. These white fellas behind the auto unions that started up this year, it's not gonna be like with the Teamsters. They want to open it up to everybody. *Colored* men'll be able to join their union—"

"Um-*umph*!" Mr. Chambers interjected. "Won't that be somethin'!"

"This'll be *our* chance to get some of those *good* factory jobs," Mr. Clark continued.

Mr. Jones broke in. "I could even go over to the Ford plant and apply—" He cut his sentence short and cut a quick glance over at Douglas Ford.

Doug's father had finished his ice cream and was packing tobacco into his pipe. He looked up from what he was doing and spoke. "Jones, you go on and get a job at Ford's if you want to. But you know as well as I do that I pay you more than they're giving out at that plant. And I pay you more money than any union's gonna get you, too. Much more. But you go on. Lots of guys around here just waitin' for your job."

The men fell silent for a long while after that. Doug was still sitting and listening over by the house. He wanted to hear more; he felt like one of the men. But his stomach was full and his arm ached. He dozed off.

When Doug woke up, his father was talking again.

"Well, I've been down there to that Teamster's union hall. They know my face by now. And they aren't lettin' any colored truckers in their union."

"Ford, you don't need that union. You're doin' better than the lot of 'em," Mr. Chambers said.

"That's right," Mr. Jones concurred.

"Naw—you don't understand. The union'd stand behind me. They'd back me up. I wouldn't need Jim Hines if I had the Teamsters behind me," Douglas Ford explained.

At the mention of that name—Jim Hines— Doug sat straight up. The bowl that had been resting between his knees crashed to the ground and shattered all around him.

His father saw what had happened out of the corner of his eye and rushed over to where Doug sat. He leaned over and said in a low voice, "Don't worry, son. I'll get a broom and help you clean this up."

Doug grabbed his father's arm. "Who's Jim Hines, Dad?"

"He's a driver, son."

"Why do you need him to work for you?"

"It's business, son."

"How does he back you up?"

"Just like I said, it's business. Now let's get this mess cleaned up."

9

Drum and Bugle Corps

Rat! Rat! Rat a tat tat. Rat! Rat! Rat a tat tat.
"C'mon, Doug! Don't you wanna be a part of the drum and bugle corps?" Henry yelled up to his friend. He and Frankie were standing just under the kitchen window.

Doug looked down at them. He spoke almost in a whisper. "I'll be out in a minute. I gotta do somethin' first."

"Well, hurry up!" Frankie added. "Mr. Black-mon's gettin' ready to start the first practice. The guys are strapping on their drums!"

Doug was in the house all alone—his mother was out back hanging wash on the clothesline. The girls were outside too. His dad was making deliveries. Doug dragged a kitchen chair to the sink.

"Why didn't I think of this before?" he asked himself. He climbed onto the chair, reached, and slowly took down his mother's big ledger from the shelf over the sink. Jim Hines was a driver, his dad had said so, so his name should be in the ledger with all of the other drivers' names. His mother kept a record of each driver, the customers he made deliveries to, how much each customer owed, and how much the customer had paid. So Jim Hines's name should be in that book.

Doug laid the ledger on the kitchen table. He carefully turned page after page. There were entries for his dad, Mr. Jones, Mr. Evert, Mr. Johnson, Mr. Katzinger, and Mr. Poniakowski. Nothing for Jim Hines, though. Nothing.

"This just doesn't make sense. Somethin's not right!" Doug mumbled to himself. His mother would be returning with the wash soon, so he put the ledger back on the shelf and dragged the chair back to the kitchen table.

Rat! Rat! Rat a tat tat. Doug ran down the back steps and joined his buddies.

"Gather 'round, gentlemen!" It was Mr. Jim Blackmon, the founder and leader of the Phillip Thomas Post Number 481 Drum and Bugle Corps.

"But I don't wanna play a drum. I wanna play a bugle," Doug whispered.

"Well, you know he makes all the new fellas start on the drum," Henry reminded him.

"Gentlemen . . ."

The drum and bugle corps used the Ford driveway for practices. It was wide enough to accommodate all of the young men—sometimes there were as many as twenty of them in the corps. It was also safer than practicing on one of the side streets. And the even planks of wood in the driveway made it easier for them to learn their marching steps and to do their drills.

"Gentlemen," Mr. Blackmon began, "it is the first weekend in May, and this is our initial practice of the season. We have a great deal of work to do before our annual Memorial Day march. And we can be ready if we work hard and put our hearts to the task."

Mr. Blackmon looked around him. "I see some new faces," he said, peering down at Frankie, Henry, Doug, and another boy—Roy, from around the block. "Are you young men twelve years old?" he asked.

"Yessir!"

"Yessir!"

"Yessir!"

Three of them answered proudly. Doug

remained silent.

"Young Mr. Ford," Mr. Blackmon said, addressing Doug, "are you twelve years old?"

"Can I play the bugle?" Doug asked sheepishly.

"Can you answer my question? How old are you?" Mr. Blackmon asked again.

"Twelve," Doug answered.

"You can join the drum and bugle corps at the age of twelve. You begin by playing the drum. The field drum," he said, nodding over to one of the snare drums that was up against the house. "If a bugler's position opens up, you may ask again then. But you have to provide your own horn." He paused. "Do you want to join the corps?"

"Yes, Mr. Blackmon," Doug answered tentatively, looking down at his feet.

Mr. Blackmon just glared at him.

Doug felt the stare. He raised his head and looked Mr. Blackmon in the eye. He answered again with conviction, "Yes, sir!"

"Then let's get you fitted," he said, looking at Doug and the three other new recruits.

Doug glanced over at the returning drummers. They all knew what to do and helped each other strap on their drums. Mr. Blackmon led the new members to their drums. He showed them how to fit the straps so that the drums sat the correct distance below the waist.

Doug could barely stand straight with the drum pulling on him. He looked at his buddies. They were being pulled down by the weight of their instruments as well.

"Heavier than you thought, eh?" Mr. Blackmon said with a smile as he looked at the boys. "You'll get used to it," he assured them. Then he handed them each a set of brand new drumsticks.

"Take care of these," he warned them. "The next set *you* pay for."

"Yessir!" they said in unison.

Boom! Boom! Boom! Boom!

"Sounds like Fred, my bass drummer, is ready," Mr. Blackmon said. Doug looked up. Fred was an older teen he had never seen before. He had a huge drum strapped to his front, but it rested sideways against his stomach. Instead of hitting the drum from the top, he hit one side and then the other with two large drumsticks that were padded at the tips. Fred strained to see over the top of the drum as he played.

Boom! Boom! Boom! Boom!

"Corpsmen, let's go!" Mr. Blackmon ordered as he blew his whistle and began marching at the front of the group. The experienced drummers filed behind him two by two.

Doug and his friends followed behind those drummers, imitating their every step. Doug glanced behind. The buglers brought up the rear, carrying their horns across their chests.

Mr. Blackmon led them up and down the driveway. Doug thought his legs would buckle beneath him. Mr. Blackmon blew his whistle once again. The corps immediately stopped. Doug and Henry, who marched side by side, crashed into the drummers ahead of them.

"Pay attention and listen for the whistle," Mr. Blackmon scolded, looking straight at the two friends.

Again, the whistle blew. Again, Mr. Blackmon bellowed, "Let's go!"

It was during a break in the middle of their practice that Doug learned the importance of those two words, "Let's go!" It was the motto of the 369th Infantry, a regiment of colored soldiers. According to Mr. Blackmon, they fought bravely alongside the French during the Great War—World War I.

"The American military let very few colored soldiers see battle," Mr. Blackmon explained. He paced back and forth before his corpsmen. "But the French were more than happy to give our colored troops a chance to fight. The French gave them uniforms. They gave them weapons, food . . . and the 369th fought *valiantly,*" he explained, still pacing before the youngsters. "*Valiantly.* In fact, they never gave up an inch of ground. They never lost a prisoner!" he declared proudly. "By the end of the war, the 369th Infantry—as well as two other colored regiments, the 371st *and* the 372nd—fought so bravely that the French government awarded all three the Croix de Guerre. That, gentlemen, is one of the highest military honors that France can bestow."

Mr. Blackmon stopped in his tracks. He looked up and down his assembly of corpsmen. "So when you hear the whistle as we begin our drills, I want the whole corps to proudly proclaim, 'Let's go!'—Let me hear it."

He sounded the whistle and began marching in place.

"Let's go!" the corps shouted.

"Once again!"

"Let's go!"

"For the 369th!"

"Let's go!"

"Men of bronze!"

"Let's go!"

Mr. Blackmon blew his whistle once again.

"Let's go!"

Even with the break, Doug, Frankie, Henry, and Roy were dog tired. But they managed to make it through their paces as the newest members of the Phillip Thomas Post Number 481 Drum and Bugle Corps.

―――――

It was the Saturday after Memorial Day. Doug wore his drum and bugle corps uniform for the first time: a flat-topped black cap with a gold cord fastened around the base of the crown. His matching black pants had a gold stripe along the outside of each leg. He tucked a crisply starched long-sleeved shirt into his pants.

He was all set to take part in the Memorial Day march. Every year the drum and bugle corps led a procession through the cemetery located a few blocks from their house. It was just off Joseph Campau Street. With neighbors from far and wide following close behind them, the corps marched to a row of white crosses that marked the graves of soldiers who had died in the Great War.

"My, but don't you look handsome!" Doug's mother exclaimed when she turned and saw him walk into the kitchen.

"Son, you've become quite a drummer since you started with the corps. And it's only been three weeks," Doug's father said, sitting at the kitchen table. "Three weeks isn't a long time. Already you're going to be in the Memorial Day march. That's really somethin'!"

His mother bent over and kissed him on the forehead. "We're proud of you, son," she said softly.

"Yeah, but I wanna play the bugle. I don't wanna be a drummer!" Doug protested.

"Well, maybe you will, son," his father replied. "The drums are fine for now."

"Mr. Blackmon says you gotta bring your own bugle," Doug explained.

"Well?" his dad asked.

"I don't have a bugle!" Doug almost shouted.

His father looked up from his breakfast. "The drums are fine for now," he repeated.

Doug wolfed down his oatmeal. He got his drum from the back porch and went into the backyard to strap it on. Pointo yelped and rushed out at him from the back of the yard.

"Sit, girl! You'll get my new uniform all dirty!"

Pointo stopped in her tracks. The dog sat and watched. Doug pulled the wide leather straps over his shoulders. He tugged and twisted the drum until it felt just right against his stomach. Then he took out his drumsticks.

Rat! Rat! Rat a tat tat. Rat! Rat! Rat a tat tat.

He practiced up and down the driveway. He heard dishes being cleared as he marched beneath the kitchen window. Patsy, Laura, and Jean even came out to watch. They sat on the back steps and stomped their feet to the drum beat. Seeing them there made Doug nervous, but he kept practicing.

"You ready, son?"

Doug jumped. The sound of his father's voice scared him.

"Yes, Daddy!"

Doug's father stepped off the porch. "C'mon, May—you don't want to make the boy late!" he called out.

The girls had already skipped to the front of the driveway.

May Ford came out holding baby Annie May. She placed her in the stroller. "There. We're all set," she announced.

The family walked down Halleck toward Joseph Campau Street. It was a sunny spring day. Many of the neighbors were outside. Some were sitting on their front porches. Some looked to be walking toward the cemetery as well.

"Hey, Doug!"

"Doug, wait up!"

It was Frankie and Henry. Frankie's limp made him waddle as he and Henry ran to catch up. Their drums bounced and bumped against their stomachs.

"You don't have your drums strapped on tight enough," Doug said when they finally caught up. "That's why they're bouncin' so much."

Boom! Boom! Boom! Boom! It was the sound of the bass drum.

"Agggh!" Doug and his friends gasped in unison.

"Do you think they'd start without us?" Henry asked.

Doug's father answered, "Why don't you boys go on up ahead just in case they're ready to get started. We'll be there shortly."

Doug ran as best he could. Henry and Frankie waddled. When they got to the cemetery, the drum and bugle corps was already lined up. Mr. Blackmon was standing in front, facing the group. He saw the boys and said, "Come on now! We're about to start. Take your places."

Roy was already there. Frankie took his position next to him. Doug and Henry stood in front of them.

Mr. Blackmon sounded the whistle.

"Let's go!" the entire corps shouted.

Boom! Boom! Boom! Boom!

Rat! Rat! Rat a tat tat. Rat! Rat! Rat a tat tat.

People lined up on both sides of the narrow gravel road. They cheered on the corps as they marched by. When the corpsmen reached the end of the road, the crowd grew quiet. There was a long row of white crosses. These marked the graves of the soldiers who had died in the Great War. The corpsmen stood at attention. One of the buglers stepped out of formation. He began to play taps. The long somber notes of the horn filled the air. Not another sound could be heard.

Then Doug heard sniffles. He looked around. Men were wiping their eyes. Women were softly crying. Someone had laid a wreath of flowers at one of the graves.

"About face!" Mr. Blackmon commanded.

The corpsmen turned and faced the opposite direction.

Mr. Blackmon sounded the whistle.

"Let's go!" the corps responded.

Boom! Boom! Boom! Boom!

The sound of the bass drum seemed to make the ground beneath them vibrate, Doug thought.

As the corps marched out, Doug passed his parents and the girls. He glanced over to where they stood among the onlookers, over to the side of the road. The crowd remained silent— some men saluted—as the Phillip Thomas Post Number 481 Drum and Bugle Corps left the cemetery.

10

Chicken in the Truck

Hee haw donkey saw! Hee haw donkey saw! It was a warm Saturday afternoon and Doug was working with his father in the wood yard. Doug stacked the wood while his dad worked the saw. He kept a stack of wood piled high close to the donkey engine. That way his father could quickly grab a plank, place it on the movable tray, and then feed it to the saw. Doug kept the wood stacked close to the saw but not too close.

"Dad, let me put the wood on the tray! I won't come near the saw blade. I'll be careful. Promise!" Doug pleaded.

His father kept working as he answered him. "Son, accidents happen quickly when you're workin' a saw. You think you're safe and the next thing you know, your finger's pretty near cut off."

He pushed the tray toward the saw. He had a slow, steady rhythm as he worked.

"Unh-unh. You're gonna be a doctor and—"

"I know, I know," Doug said finishing the sentence, "a doctor needs *all* his fingers."

They both smiled.

Hee haw donkey saw! Hee haw donkey saw!
His father didn't talk a lot when he was working the saw. Doug understood that it was dangerous work and his dad needed to concentrate. But there was something on his mind, and he wanted to talk about it. He wanted to talk about Jim Hines.

"Dad," he said above the noise. His father didn't reply.

"Dad!" he said again.

"Mm hm."

"Dad, I don't understand about Jim Hines. Is he a good man or not? Does he help you or not? Sometimes it sounds like—"

His father cut him off before he could finish his sentence.

"Son, Jim Hines is like everyone else. He has his good side and his bad side. But I'll tell you this: I wouldn't be in this business without him. The Douglas Ford Wood Company would not exist without Jim Hines!"

"But I don't understand," Doug said. "Ever

since I was a little boy I've seen everybody else in your business. All your drivers." He rattled off the names of Jones, Evert, Poniakowski, Johnson, and Katzinger. "But I only *hear* about Jim Hines—I've never seen him. How come?" Doug was pleading now. "You let me make deliveries with you. You let me stack the wood for the saw. I'm older now. I'm old enough to know. Who's Jim Hines, Dad? Who is he?"

His father didn't answer. He was silent and kept working the saw. Doug had even more questions, but he knew not to ask them then. He focused on his work and kept stacking the wood.

———

Since it was Saturday, more often than not that meant May Ford would be fixing fried chicken for dinner. Covered in flour and seasoned with salt, pepper, and paprika, the chicken frying in the skillet was one of the best smells in the world, Doug thought. His mother wouldn't stand for anything but the freshest chicken. That meant going to the poultry market and bringing home a live chicken still clucking in a burlap bag. Using the skills she picked up growing up in Clarksville, Tennessee, Doug's mother swiftly broke the chicken's neck. Then, she carefully plucked off the feathers, pulled out its insides, and commenced to cutting. The rest of the dinner would be biscuits, gravy, and maybe string beans or collard greens. Doug's mouth watered just thinking about it!

Sure enough, later that afternoon, Douglas Ford stood next to his truck and called for the children. "Who's going with me to get the chicken?"

"Me!" "I am!" "I am!" "Me, too!" Doug and the girls came running from all parts of the backyard and the house. They climbed up the side board and squeezed into the cab of the truck. May Ford and baby Annie May watched from the driveway as they headed out.

The poultry market was in Black Bottom. That was the section of Detroit where most of the colored families lived. There were a number of colored businesses near where Doug and his family lived on Dequindre and Davison—Dr. Hammonds's office; their church, Gideon AME Zion; and Shorty's. There was also Mr. Allen's print shop. He printed up the bulletins for a lot of the colored churches in the city. He also did wedding invitations and funeral programs. There was even a colored dentist, Dr. Martin.

But most of the colored businesses were in Black Bottom, and that's where Douglas Ford went to get his chickens. He could've gone over on Joseph Campau Street and gotten one in Hamtramck, and sometimes he did. But most times that Doug could remember, his dad just piled all the kids into the truck and went a few miles down Dequindre to Forest Avenue and then over to McDougall to the poultry market down there.

"Here, Doug," Douglas Ford said as he opened the truck door and got back in behind the steering wheel. He had gone in the market by himself. But as usual, once he got back to the car, he handed his son the burlap bag with the live chicken inside. "Hold on tight!" he chuckled.

The girls squealed as the chicken squawked and tried to flap its wings inside the bag.

"Quiet down, girls," their father said as he settled in.

"The chicken's peckin' me, dad," Doug complained.

"Come on, now. We'll be home before you know it," he answered.

But the ride home didn't get off to such a good start. The chicken kept pecking at Doug's arms and chest. He pushed the bag onto the floor of the cab, but then the chicken started pecking the girls' legs, and they started screaming and kicking.

"Settle down, children!" Douglas Ford ordered. "Doug, hold onto that chicken!"

Then somehow, some way, the string that tied the burlap bag closed came loose and the chicken got out. There were wings flapping, kids screaming, arms flailing.

"Holy Christmas!" their father shouted, and then he started coughing because there were chicken feathers in the air and they were floating all around his mouth and nose. He turned off the main road and managed to pull the truck over to the side of a street lined with brick row houses. Doug could tell by all of the colored folks he saw sitting on porches and walking by on the sidewalk that they were still in Black Bottom.

It didn't take long for a crowd to form around the truck. Onlookers pointed and watched as Doug tried to hold open the bag while his father struggled to get the flapping, pecking chicken

105

back into it. The girls were still screaming, and all of them were coughing because of the chicken feathers in the air. Doug could hear some folks saying, "What's goin' on in there?" "Is he hurting those kids?" "Are those his children?" "Should someone call the police?"

Finally, they got the chicken back in the bag. Doug's father tied the bag shut tight. Folks backed away as he got out of the cab carrying the burlap bag. He threw the chicken into the back of the truck where he hauled the wood and tied it down.

"Is everything all right?" "Are those your kids?" "Are they OK?"

"Yes, yes, we're fine. The chicken got loose is all. Those are my children. They're fine," he answered them all at once.

Then came a man's surly voice above the others. Doug heard it from where he sat in the cab. He couldn't quite make out what the man said. He turned and looked out the window. The girls leaned up against him and watched too.

The man continued, "Their mother must be pretty high yellow for you to be the daddy of brown-skinned young 'uns like that. I bet their mama's got some nice, long hair. Good hair . . ."

There was a gasp in the crowd. Doug's father, still outside the truck, turned in the direction of the voice.

"A dark-skinned gal's not good enough for you, huh?" the man asked.

Doug's father didn't answer.

"I said . . ." the man continued.

"I heard you," Douglas Ford said flatly.

By then he had found the man's face and stared him down. "I won't have that kinda talk in front of my children." He spoke methodically. "You have anything to say about my family, you say it to me in private. In fact, we can step over there to the side and talk about it right now if you'd like."

Doug knew his father wouldn't fight. His father didn't believe in fighting. He had often preached to the children against it. He said there was always a better way to work things out. But the man didn't know that about his father. The man backed down. Doug heard him mumble something and walk away. His father stood there by the truck for a while, following the man with his eyes. Then he got back behind the steering wheel and started the engine. They pulled off, and Doug watched from the window as the crowd broke up. The girls sat stock still in the cab and didn't say a word. It was a long, quiet ride home.

11

Riding to the Factory

Vroom-vroom. Vroom-vroom. Vroom-vroom. The men were coming to work. Doug heard the rumbling sound of their engines as they headed up Halleck Street toward the wood yard.

He stood by the kitchen stove to warm himself. It was early summer, but the mornings were still chilly. He rubbed his hands together. He was waiting for his mother to come into the kitchen and start the oatmeal. School was out for the summer, so his sisters slept in. But Doug had gotten up early, as usual, to start the fire in the kitchen stove. He was hungry. He wanted his hot oatmeal.

Vroom-vroom. Vroom-vroom. Doug ran to the kitchen window. He watched Mr. Katzinger and Mr. Evert drive up in their pickup trucks. Mr. Jones walked up the driveway.

"Daddy, they're here!" he announced to his father. "Mr. Jones is walking. I think he'll need to drive one of *your* trucks today," he added.

His father didn't answer. He could hear his parents' muffled voices from their bedroom off the dining room. Doug went and stood by the dining-room table, pretending to look through one of his books. But he was really straining to hear what his parents were saying.

"Oh, Douglas," his mother said. "Why now? There's plenty of time for him to find out."

"You haven't heard him, I have. He's thinkin' about it, I can tell. He's been askin' over and over, May, over and over."

"Jim Hines," Doug thought anxiously, "they've gotta be talkin' about Jim Hines!"

"He's at that age," his father continued. "He'll figure it out one day on his own. Might as well tell him now. Don't worry, he's ready—I can tell."

"But he's so young—"

"May, I've made up my mind. I know what I'm doin'. It's time he knew!"

Doug cocked his head toward the door trying to hear more, but they had finished talking. He quietly ran back into the kitchen.

May Ford opened their bedroom door. "Who's hungry?" she asked as she walked through the dining room. She was holding Annie May in her arms. She handed the baby over to Doug as she entered the kitchen.

As he held his sister, Doug turned toward the kitchen window to watch the drivers. Mr. Poniakowski was there now. So was Mr. Johnson. For several minutes Doug watched as they huddled together by one of the trucks. He could hear the sound of his mother in the background stirring the pot of oatmeal.

"Son, school's out. You'll go with me to the factory this morning," Doug's father announced as he walked into the kitchen. "You'll have to eat pretty fast now—"

Doug stood there with his mouth hanging open. He couldn't believe what he was hearing. "Really, Dad? Really?" he was finally able to get the words out. "But what do I do?" he asked his father anxiously. "How will I know what to do?"

"Just do as I do, you'll be fine," he answered. "Make sure you bring your work gloves. May, what about that oatmeal?"

Doug put the baby in the high chair. He took his seat. His mother spooned steaming-hot oatmeal into their bowls. Doug sprinkled cinnamon on his, and then he ate quickly. Even so, his

111

father was already standing before Doug could
finish eating.

"Let's go, son!" he said tapping Doug on the
shoulder. He kissed his wife on the top of her
head and then went out the back door.

Doug looked over at his mother as she fed
Annie May.

"You do as your father says, you hear me?"
she instructed.

"I will," Doug promised. "Where'd I put my
gloves?"

"On the back porch."

Doug was up and out the door. He found his
gloves. His father was giving the drivers their
orders when Doug joined him at the truck.

"Let's go, son," his father said as they climbed
into the truck cab.

Doug's eyes were bright. He was excited. It
seemed to him that he'd been waiting his whole
life for this moment. Now it was really happen-
ing—he was going to the factory! Doug looked
over at his dad. "I can't wait to hear when you
tell everybody that I'm your son. That I'm Douglas Ford Jr.!" he said.

But his father kept his eyes on the road and
didn't say a word. As they drove down Dequin-

dre Road, they passed Dr. Hammonds's store-
front office. "One day," Doug's father began,
nodding toward the doctor's office, "one day
you'll be one of the colored doctors. *Your* name'll
be over the door like that sign for Dr. Hammonds. Douglas Ford Jr., MD, that's what it'll
say."

"Uh-huh. Right. But what about it, Dad? Are
you gonna tell everybody that I'm your son?
That I'm Douglas Ford Jr.?" Doug asked eagerly.

The traffic light was red. Douglas Ford
stopped the truck. He looked over at his son.
"Can't do that," he responded.

"Wh—what do you mean?" Doug almost stut-
tered. "Why not?"

"They don't know I'm Douglas Ford," his
father said flatly. "They don't know that I own
the wood company."

Doug leaned toward his dad. "They *have* to
know. You're the owner of the Douglas Ford
Wood Company. You have a wood yard. You
drive up in one of your trucks. They—"

His father cut him off and looked deep into
Doug's eyes. "Yes, you know that, and our neighbors know that, and my drivers know that. But at
the factories—where I get my wood—they don't

113

know I'm the owner, Douglas Ford. And my customers that order the wood, they don't know I'm Douglas Ford, either. They know me as . . ." He stopped and took a deep breath. "Well, they know me as Jim Hines, a driver for the Douglas Ford Wood Company." The driver behind them laid on his horn. The light had turned green. Douglas Ford turned back to the road. He changed gears and the truck lurched forward.

"Jim Hines? Whadda you talkin' about? You can't be Jim Hines! C'mon, Daddy. You're jokin' with me!" Doug said, almost yelling at his father.

"They know me as Jim Hines," his father repeated.

"You're Jim Hines?" Doug was screaming now.

"Yes, I'm Jim Hines." His father's voice was steady. "Now calm down, son." He spoke deliberately. "Let me tell you how it happened—"

"No, Daddy . . . no . . ." he interrupted.

"Shhhhh . . ." Douglas Ford hushed him. Then he continued, talking while he drove, "When I came to Detroit and decided to start a business with my truck, I already knew that the Teamsters didn't want any colored truckers to be part of their union. That was fine. I didn't need to be a part of a union to be able to drive a truck."

Doug was breathing heavy now. Fast and heavy.

"Are you listening?" his father asked him.

Doug nodded his head. He couldn't say anything. He couldn't look at his father. He just stared straight ahead.

"The problem was," his dad continued, "how would I get my truck into those factories to get to that scrap wood? If they thought that I—a *colored* man—owned the business, they never would have put the Douglas Ford Wood Company on the list of businesses that can go in and get that scrap wood. That's just how it is for colored folks right now. For me to get past those gates, they had to think that the owner of the Douglas Ford Wood Company was a white man. That's how it is at all of the factories. *All* of 'em, son. Every single last one of 'em."

"But Dad it's *your* business. *You* have the wood yard. *You* have the trucks."

There was a long silence.

Doug was still breathing fast, still staring at the road ahead. He finally spoke. "Why didn't you tell me this before? Why didn't you tell me you're Jim Hines?"

"You're old enough to know now," his father answered. "It's time you knew."

There was another long silence between them.

Tears welled up in Doug's eyes. He finally spoke, his voice quivering. "So what . . . so what did you do?"

His father explained, "There was a white fella from the neighborhood. Nice guy. He was willing to help me out. I asked him to go with me one morning. Had him drive the truck. It was my first truck." He stopped and smiled. "Anyway, we drove to the loading gates of each of the car factories. I was sitting on the passenger side just like you are right now." He paused and chuckled to himself. "He told them *he* was Douglas Ford, owner of the Douglas Ford Wood Company. Asked them to put the company name on the list they kept there at the guardhouse. Then he pointed at me. Said I was his driver, Jim Hines. That I would be comin' to pick up scrap wood. That's all it took."

His father took a sharp turn. Doug grabbed the dashboard to keep from falling against the steering wheel.

Then he looked over at his dad and asked,

"What about Mr. Jones, Mr. Evert, Mr. Johnson, they're colored—"

"When they pull up, all they have to say is that they're drivers for the Douglas Ford Wood Company. The company name's already on the list. The guards let them right in. Don't you see? I'm the one that has to be Jim Hines *because I can't let them know I'm the owner.*"

Tears streamed down Doug's cheeks. "But Daddy—that's why I always wanted to go out with you. To tell everybody that I was your son. That my daddy was the owner of the Douglas Ford Wood Company." He was choked up. He couldn't say more.

"It can't happen that way. That just can't be," Douglas Ford said with a soothing tone, glancing over at him. Then he suddenly changed his voice. "We're almost at the gate. Buck up, now!" he said sternly.

Doug wiped the tears from his face with his sleeve. He sat up straight. His father pulled up to the guardhouse.

"Jim Hines for the Douglas Ford Wood Company," his dad said crisply.

Doug cringed inside when he heard those words.

The guard standing inside the booth barely glanced their way. He waved them in.

His father pulled the truck over to a huge pile of empty wooden crates. Some were still whole. Some were already broken into what looked like pallets.

"C'mon now, son, you gotta work. That's why we're here. *This* is the business, not the name. Not my name, not your name. Now get your gloves on and let's go," Doug's father said.

His dad got out of the cab and went to the truck bed. He grabbed two crowbars, one in each hand. Doug was out of the truck and pulling on his gloves by then. He took the crowbar his father handed him. He slowly followed him to where the crates were stacked. He tried not to cry, but the tears were welling up in his eyes. His father's voice filled his head, "I'm Jim Hines . . . They know me as Jim Hines . . ."

"Now watch," his father ordered, looking back at Doug.

Doug looked on as his father held a crate steady with one foot while he braced himself firmly against the ground with the other. Then he took the crowbar and loosened the boards before pulling the crate apart with his gloved

118

hands. Splinters flew through the air as he worked. Nails, too. Doug covered his eyes with his sleeve.

"Your turn," his father said, pointing over to a pile of pallets. "You try pulling those apart."

Doug set to work. No time to think about Jim Hines. He tried to brace himself as he had seen his father do. He fell backward, landing flat on the seat of his pants. He kept trying to loosen the boards with the crowbar and then with his hands. He fell backward several times.

His dad looked over his way. "You're doin' fine, son. You're gettin' the hang of it," he assured him.

Doug didn't feel like he was getting the hang of anything. By the time he had pulled apart a couple of pallets, his hands were burning. He took off his gloves. His hands were full of splinters. He had more splinters than he got stacking wood by his dad's saw at the wood yard. And he even had more than he got making deliveries and loading the wood down those chutes. His fingers and the palms of his hands felt raw. Then he looked over at the truck. He couldn't believe what he saw—his father had practically filled the entire truck bed with slats of wood.

"How's he do it?" Doug asked himself, still looking down at his hands.

"Lemme see," his father said as he walked over to where Doug stood. He took Doug's hands in his own and looked at them closely. "We'll soak 'em in vinegar and water when we get home. Those splinters'll come right out," he assured him.

His hands were throbbing now. He blew on them. He shook them. Nothing seemed to help.

"You go sit in the car. I'll fill up the truck and we'll head on back," his father said.

Doug was happy to obey. He climbed into his seat. He was exhausted, and his hands stung even worse, but as he lay his head back, a warm breeze blew against his face. He looked over at his dad. He looked over at the guardhouse. And he fell asleep.

The dreams came quickly. Frankie and Henry were running through the alley.

"Your daddy's Jim Hines! Your daddy's Jim Hines!" they teased him.

"So what if he is!" Doug yelled right back. "He's still the owner of the Douglas Ford Wood Company!"

He walked over to the saw. His father was

standing there, cutting up the boards of wood they had brought home that day.

"Why didn't you tell me, Daddy? Why didn't you tell me before?" he asked him over and over. His father didn't answer. "Why didn't you tell me?" His dad kept cutting the wood with the saw.

"So now you know, son," his father finally said, steadily working.

Vroom-vroom. Vroom-vroom. Vroom-vroom. Doug could hear the truck in his sleep.

"Wake up, son," Douglas Ford said as they made it up the driveway. He shook Doug by the arm. "Wake up. We're home now."

Doug sat up straight. He looked around at the saw, the wood pile, the trucks. The girls were playing tag in the backyard. Pointo chased behind them, yelping.

They were back home.

12

Good Service at a Fair Price

My dad is Jim Hines. My dad is Jim Hines.

That's what Doug wanted to say to Frankie and Henry when they came over that afternoon. They asked him lots of questions: "What did you do?" "Was it hard work?" "Did you talk to anybody?" "When're ya going back?"

And all Doug wanted to say was, *My dad is Jim Hines.*

But he didn't dare. They couldn't know, at least not from him.

So he answered, "I pulled apart these great big crates. My dad gave me a crowbar." Then he held out his hands. "Look!"

"Aghhh!" They both sucked in their breath.

"What happened to your hands?" Frankie asked, staring down at Doug's swollen, blistered palms.

"You shoulda seen 'em when I first got home. They were full of splinters. I soaked 'em in

122

vinegar and water."

"P-U!" Henry cried.

"Yeah, but it worked. The splinters're all gone now," Doug replied, looking down at his hands.

"You pulled 'em out?" Henry asked.

"Naw, my ma mostly," Doug answered.

The three boys stared at Doug's hands for a while more.

"So whadda you wanna do?" Frankie asked. "Play some ball?"

"I can't," Doug said. "My hands're too sore."

"So what's there to do?" Henry asked. "Marbles?"

"Nah—you know I don't like marbles," Frankie replied.

"Maybe it's 'cause you don't have any!" Henry taunted.

"Oh yeah? I got better ones than you!" Frankie asserted.

"Then lemme see 'em," Henry said.

"Come on down t' my house," Frankie said. "You too, Doug. I'll show you guys some marbles."

Doug shook his head. "You guys go on. I'm gonna stay home. Like I said, my hands're too sore."

He walked with them to the end of the driveway. He watched as they took off and ran toward Frankie's house. Then he heard the trucks. He turned and saw them coming down Halleck Street. They honked their horns. He backed himself against the side of the house as they turned into the driveway. Mr. Poniakowski, Mr. Evert, Mr. Katzinger—just three of them at first. They jumped out of their trucks. Mr. Katzinger was the first to speak.

"How was your first day at the factory?" he asked Doug.

"Fine," Doug answered.

"When's that sign over the wood yard gonna read 'Douglas Ford *and Son* Wood Company'?" Mr. Katzinger asked with a wink.

Mr. Evert answered, "C'mon, now—you know that boy's gonna be a doctor!" Then he added with a chuckle, "But I don't think he's gonna be unloading any wood today—"

"He did fine, just fine," Doug's father said, heading toward the saw. Doug hadn't seen or heard him coming.

"He got a handful of splinters I bet," Mr. Poniakowski said.

"We all did at first," his dad reminded him and

124

started his saw.

The noise from the saw stopped the talk. The men went to work unloading their trucks, piling the wood over by the saw. Doug just stood to the side and watched. He told himself he was just staying out of the way, but he and the others knew that he couldn't have helped even if he had wanted to. His hands were in pretty bad shape.

Mr. Jones pulled up. "Jones, go get the orders from my wife," Douglas Ford instructed. "The ones for this afternoon."

By the time Mr. Jones returned with a handful of orders, Mr. Johnson had pulled up too. Doug's father turned off the saw. He waved Mr. Jones over to him and took the papers. "Come over here, fellas," he called out. He handed out delivery slips. "Mt. Clemens, Grosse Pointe, Dearborn," he named the cities as he passed out the orders.

"OK, fellas, hit the road!"

The men hurried to fill their trucks with the wood Douglas Ford had cut at the saw. Pointo barked in the background as they turned their engines back on and headed on out. Doug's father returned to his saw and got back to work.

Doug stood by the side of the house, under

the kitchen window. He heard his sisters giggling above him, but he didn't look up. "Want s'more vinegar, Doug?" Patsy teased him. The girls giggled again. Doug heard his mother say, "Shhhh . . . you girls shush! And get away from that window."

His hands still burned. And now the skin felt tight. He watched his father steadily working the saw. *My dad is Jim Hines. My dad is Jim Hines.* The words came back into his head, along with the pain. It seemed the pain he felt knowing his dad was Jim Hines was as bad as his throbbing hands. He was so proud of his dad and the business. He was proud to be able to work for his dad. He wanted everybody to know that Douglas Ford was his father. Then his heart sank. He understood that they could never know. If people knew his father was the owner of the Douglas Ford Wood Company, he wouldn't get any wood from the factories. No wood, no deliveries, no business. It made sense, but it still didn't seem right. And he still felt the pain.

Doug spoke up. "Aren't you goin' out on deliveries today?" he asked his father.

"Not today," he answered. "They can handle it without me."

Doug stepped away from the house. He started to say something and then stopped. He opened his mouth but still didn't say anything.

"Got somethin' on your mind, son?" Douglas Ford asked. He stopped his saw.

"Well, Dad, I was wonderin'. . ."

"Yep?"

"When I'm a doctor, will I have to pretend to be somebody else?"

"No, son. You'll have plenty of patients. Lots of colored folks will need a good doctor."

"White folks won't come to a colored doctor?" Doug asked.

"Maybe some will one day. But you'll have plenty of colored patients to keep you busy. Mark my word," his dad assured him.

"So why do you need to be Jim Hines? Aren't there enough colored folks around to buy your wood?"

"Afraid not, son. I've got to be able to sell wood far and wide to keep the business going. Listen," he explained. "Your mother puts nice ads in the paper. Folks read 'em, call in, place an order. I give good service at a fair price, and they keep callin' back. Now a few wouldn't mind buying wood from a colored business. Our Pol-

ish neighbors come down with their wheelbar-
rows and buy wood from me all the time. But
most folks wouldn't buy a stick from me if they
knew a colored man owned the business. That's
just how it is," he answered.

Doug looked down at the driveway.

"Look at me," his father continued. Doug
turned his head. "I'm makin' a good living even
in this depression. I help a few others make a
good living too." He paused and then added,
"This Jim Hines thing? It's what I have to do."

Then Doug blurted out, "But what if somebody tells?"

"Who's gonna tell?" he answered. "One of the
drivers? Naw—they'd be out of a job. A few of
the neighbors know, but they know how important this wood yard is to too many people. They
keep it to themselves."

He stepped closer to Doug and looked him
square in the eyes. "I know it doesn't seem right.
But you'll understand better one day. Now let's
take a look at those hands."

Doug pulled them out of his pockets and
opened up his palms.

"Hmmm . . ." his dad examined them on both
sides. "You put in a good day's work, son. You

think those hands of yours could hold a bar-beque sandwich?"

Doug looked up at his father. "They sure could!" he exclaimed. His eyes got bright. He knew just what his father was talking about. There was a barbeque place not far from the chicken market. Down in Black Bottom. Doug loved their pulled-pork sandwiches, dripping with sauce, with a side order of coleslaw.

"Let's go see what your mother and the girls think about me bringing home a big sack of sandwiches!"

Doug followed his dad in the house. His mother was on the telephone. She was taking down an order.

"Thank you very much, Mr. Sampson. Yes, I will . . . yes . . . I'll be sure and tell him." She hung up the phone. "Mr. Sampson just placed an order for a half cord of wood."

"Good customer," Douglas Ford answered.

"And he had a message for Jim Hines."

Doug cast down his eyes, his shoulders slumped.

"He said to tell Mr. Ford that his driver Jim Hines always sweeps up after a delivery. He appreciates that," she said.

129

"Give 'em good service at a fair price," his father replied. He looked over at Doug, "Right, son?"

Doug straightened his shoulders. He looked his dad—the owner of the Douglas Ford Wood Company—straight in the eyes. He could see his father at the donkey saw, behind the wheel of the truck making deliveries, and handing out delivery orders to the drivers. He pictured him breaking down crates at the factory and giving him and his buddies special wood for their scooters and wagons.

"Right, son?"

And with pride in his voice, Doug answered, "That's right, Dad, good service at a fair price and they keep callin' back!"

Epilogue

The Douglas Ford Wood Company died a natural death after World War II. By that time most homes had converted to oil- and gas-powered furnaces as well as gas and electric stoves. It was then that Douglas Ford Sr. began working for Long Manufacturing, an auto parts supplier located in his neighborhood. A few years later, he took a job at the Chrysler Corporation, where he remained for ten years until illness forced him to retire.

Douglas Ford Jr. earned his medical degree from Meharry Medical School in 1951 and became a pediatrician. He practiced medicine in Montclair, New Jersey, for almost fifty years. His sisters all earned their bachelors and masters degrees and taught in the Detroit Public Schools.

No one—other than members of the immediate family, the drivers, and a few close friends— ever knew the true identity of Jim Hines.

About the Author

Jean Alicia Elster (BA, University of Michigan; JD, University of Detroit) is the author of the children's book series Joe Joe in the City, which includes the books *Just Call Me Joe Joe* (2001), *I Have a Dream, Too!* (2002), *I'll Fly My Own Plane* (2002), and *I'll Do the Right Thing* (2004). Elster was awarded the 2002 Governors' Emerging Artist Award by ArtServe Michigan for her work in the series, and in 2004, *I'll Do the Right Thing* received the Atlanta Daily World Choice Award in the category of children's books.

Elster has also edited several books, including *The Death Penalty, The Outbreak of the Civil War,* and *Building Up Zion's Walls: Ministry for Empowering the African American Family.* Her essays have appeared in many national publications, including *Ms., World Vision, Black Child,* and *Christian Scientist Sentinel.* She also collaborated in the preparation of the manuscript for *Dear Mrs. Parks: A Dialog with Today's Youth,* by Rosa Parks, which was honored with four awards, including the NAACP Image Award and the Teacher's Choice Award.

In recognition of her outstanding work, Elster was awarded residencies at the internationally acclaimed Ragdale Foundation in Lake Forest, Illinois, in 2001, 2003, and 2005.

Elster lives in Detroit, Michigan, with her husband and two children.

.